**JEFF'S**

"You're different, Sara," Jeff smiled at her, and Sara knew he meant it as a compliment.

"I'd like to go out with you again," he said, placing his hands lightly on Sara's shoulders. Then, just as surely as if this weren't their first kiss, Jeff lowered his head and touched his lips to hers.

ANNE REYNOLDS is the pseudonym for a writer who lives with her husband and two children in New York, USA.

# Jeff's New Girl

## Anne Reynolds

**HODDER AND STOUGHTON**

For *Elizabeth*, because you believed; and *Joanne*, for your help.

Copyright © 1984 by Ann E. Steinke

First published in the USA by New American Library, 1984

First published in Great Britain by Lightning Books, 1988

MAGIC MOMENTS™ is a registered trade mark

**British Library C.I.P.**

Reynolds, Anne
Jeff's new girl.
I. Title  II. Series
813'.54[F]

ISBN 0-340-48496-9

Printed and bound in Great Britain for Hodder and Stoughton Paperbacks, a division of Hodder and Stoughton Ltd., Mill Road, Dunton Green, Sevenoaks, Kent TN13 2YA (Editorial Office: 47 Bedford Square, London WC1B 3DP) by Richard Clay Ltd., Bungay, Suffolk.

# 1

It was like Winnie the Pooh's blustery day. Rain had been falling on Carteret Island for the last two days as if it were trying to break a record for the month of March. The wet straw-colored marshlands looked so uninviting even a duck wouldn't want to live there. The temperature was in the low fifties but it felt colder.

Thinking about the weather made Sara snuggle deeper under the patchwork quilt her grandmother had made, and wish she could stay in bed all day. But she knew any minute she'd hear her mom's voice calling up the stairs. In this house no one was allowed to stay in bed except Gram, who had a touch of arthritis. Everyone had chores to do and was expected to do them without grumbling—at least not out loud. Even little five-year-old Joy had work. Sara could see her small curly-haired form huddled under her own little quilt against the far side of her bed.

If there was one thing Sara wanted more than anything else she could think of in this world it was her own room like she'd had before Joy was born. But there were only three bedrooms in the Wilsons' old two-story house. They were all on the second floor, along with an ancient bathroom. One bedroom was her parents' and one Gram's, leaving the third for the girls.

Downstairs was a kitchen with a huge pantry, a dining room, a living room, and an old-fashioned parlor. There had been talk of turning the parlor into a room for Gram and separating the girls, but so far that had been only a source of discussion, not action.

Sara sighed, stretched, and told herself for the millionth time it didn't matter. She loved Joy. The whole family did. After the Wilsons had given up on ever having another child after Sara, Joy had come along. The first time Mr. Wilson held her in his arms, he'd said, "Our little surprise bundle of joy," and that's how Joy had gotten her name.

Joy was sweet, Sara conceded. Always laughing and playing. The trouble was, her playthings were constantly strewn all over *their* room, and Sara had to continually watch her step for fear she'd either trip over something or break a favorite toy.

She peered over the edge of her bed now to see what she had to avoid when she got up.

"It's a miracle," she murmured as she saw a clear path across the wide-board flooring from her bed to the dresser.

"Sara!" her mother yelled up the stairs. Sara knew it must be eight o'clock, the latest she was allowed to sleep on Sunday.

"Yes, Mom," she answered, knowing exactly what would come next.

"Time to get up. And get Joy up."

With a groan Sara flung the cozy covers back and

swung her feet to the floor. "Joy?" she called, and went to the bed.

There was no sign Joy had heard her, but Sara knew she had. It was part of their morning game. She reached out, pulled at Joy's little quilt, and was rewarded with a giggle. "Come on, lazybones. Up."

Sara began tickling her sister, who shrieked and scrambled up to get away from her tormentor. Then she flung herself into Sara's waiting arms and they hugged. Sara smiled into Joy's neck. She smelled of baby powder. Gently Sara lowered Joy to the floor and the little girl scampered away to the old oak bureau to pull out her clothes. Joy's drawers were the bottom two; Sara's, the top three.

After Joy had tugged her clothes out and bounced onto Sara's bed to dress, Sara selected some jeans and a plaid blouse and headed for the bathroom. At sixteen she was far too physically developed to undress in the same room with her little sister. Joy couldn't understand why it was okay for her to be seen without any clothes on by Sara, but not the other way around. But at least she accepted it with the same sweet innocence that she accepted everything else in her small life.

Sara allowed herself a wistful moment to yearn for her very own room in which she could stand stark naked if she wanted to, and then told herself to stop feeling sorry for herself. She went into the bathroom and closed the door.

After she'd put on the well-worn jeans and the blouse with its slightly frayed collar, she looked at herself in the mirror, making a face. She hoped it wasn't true that clothes made the man, because hers were the pits. Money wasn't something this family had a lot of, so clothes were mended until they looked like the patchwork quilts Gram had sewn for everyone's bed. It was just as well, Sara thought. She wasn't anything special either.

Her mother insisted she was adorable. Sara disagreed. She felt sure Joy had inherited all the "adorable" genes and Sara had gotten the "chipmunk-cheek" ones. And her nose—a little more of an upturn and it would have looked just like one of her father's fishing hooks! Mrs. Wilson also maintained that Sara was overreacting to her nose, that those cheeks were simply high cheekbones temporarily covered by baby fat and soon the fat would melt away and the bones would win out. Sara had been waiting for that to happen for the past year, and as far as she could tell, the baby fat was still winning the war.

She tried sucking in her cheeks while she brushed the cap of short auburn hair on her head until it gleamed. She decided she didn't look too bad with sunken cheeks. The trouble was, she couldn't possibly walk around all day with her cheeks sucked in. Especially since it made her mouth look like she'd just eaten twenty lemons.

With a moan of defeat Sara let her cheeks out and went down the well-polished stairs, trailing her hand down the gleaming maple banister. They might not have much money, but her mom worked hard to keep what they did have spic and span. She turned at the bottom of the stairs and caught a look at herself in the mirror on the wall at the base. She knew her face wasn't that bad, but it really didn't matter whether she was cute or not. She'd had as many dates as she had fingers on one hand, but none of the boys had exactly acted like if she died tomorrow their lives would be unbearable.

She turned and headed down the hall toward the kitchen. Joy was there ahead of her, folding the napkins and placing them next to the silverware she'd already put on the table. Her job was to handle the plastic and metal things, while Sara was in charge of the glass and china.

Mrs. Wilson stopped in her task of draining sausage on a paper towel and looked at Sara. "Sara, will you make two apple pies after breakfast? I want them for dessert when the Moores are here."

"Yes," Sara said automatically, and then thought: Oh, no! She'd completely forgotten this was the one Sunday of the month her family got together with their friends for the midday meal. Unless the fish were nasty enough to choose that very day to go on a full-scale run out in the channel. Then all the fishermen on Carteret Island raced out in their boats to try to catch as many as possible before they disappeared. That was how they made their living and that came before all else. Today there weren't any fish begging to be caught, so the Wilson family was getting together with the Moores as usual. Jim Moore, a fellow professional fisherman, had been Tom Wilson's friend before either had married, and the two families' monthly get-together had been a part of Sara's life as far back as she could remember.

Yuck! Sara thought now as she glanced out the window at that awful monsoon. What a wonderful day this was going to be. Because of the weather, there would be three boys aged seventeen, ten, and nine, plus two girls, aged sixteen and five, cooped up in the house with five adults. She could just see it. The younger boys, Robbie and Stewart, would no doubt keep themselves occupied snooping around the girls' room, trying to find Sara's diary or anything else they could use at a future date to blackmail her with. Poor little Joy would drag out all her baby toys and wonder why they didn't want to play with them. As the afternoon wore on, the boys would get more and more restless, complaining about the weather. They would nag to go out, even if it was raining, because what they really wanted to be doing was fishing off the dock or hunting snakes in the field across the road. Sara thought it was a pity there weren't any boa constrictors on the island for them to play with.

At least she could look forward to playing some board

games with Jeff to help relieve her misery. Jeff was seventeen and there were occasions when she was sure he didn't feature spending time with a sixteen-year-old girl he'd known all his life, but whenever they got together Gram would make suggestions like, "Why don't you and Jeff go play checkers?" Or, "Why don't you two go out in a boat?" Jeff would always agree, although Sara wondered if he did it to be nice rather than because he wanted to. But then, what choice did he have? Actually, once they got going on a game, they always had a great time. And on a day when it looked like they could all end up in lifeboats, it was a good thing there were plenty of games to keep them going.

Sara heaved a deep sigh. Her mother shot her a quick look.

"Didn't you sleep well last night?" she inquired.

"Huh?" Sara snapped out of it as she stared at her mom.

"You sighed like you're tired," her mother explained, studying her closely.

"Oh, yeah. I slept okay." Sara finished setting the white porcelain plates with their cobalt-blue edging at the five places around the table.

Mrs. Wilson stood at a white-porcelain-enameled gas range. It was, as Gram liked to say, "as old as the hills." But since it was huge and had enough room to cook a large number of things on it or in it at the same time, she insisted she didn't want a new one. Sara watched her brush a damp lock of brown hair away from her forehead, and felt a strange restlessness inside. There was something about seeing her mom in this familiar setting, cooking and getting hot from the effort, that made Sara feel unsettled. She tried to put it into words.

"Mom? Have you ever felt like you're missing something?"

"All the time," Mrs. Wilson said with a laugh.

"No, I mean, like there's a great big hole in your life and you don't know how to fill it?"

Her mother gave Sara a skeptical look and glanced around the kitchen at the mess that came with breakfast preparation. "No," she said flatly and a little tiredly.

Sara knew what she was thinking. Her mother had so much work she never had time to think about holes in her life. But even though Sara, too, had plenty of chores and schoolwork to keep her busy, still she felt this strange emptiness. She tried again to explain it.

"Well, I do. I feel as if I'm . . . well, kind of waiting for something to happen. And I don't know what it is."

Mrs. Wilson stared at her daughter, her brow creased. She went back to breaking eggs into the black cast-iron skillet and turned down the heat of the old gas stove. "What do you mean by that, Sara?" She sounded perplexed.

Sara let out a ragged breath and walked to the refrigerator to get out the orange juice. "Oh, nothing," she said softly, and began pouring juice into everyone's glass.

It was no use. Her mother just couldn't understand. And she didn't really blame her; Sara couldn't understand what was the matter with herself either.

The door of the screened-in porch off the back of the house banged open and a couple of seconds later Mr. Wilson filled the doorway to the kitchen. He was a big gruff man with a weathered, blunted face from spending many hours out in the sun and wind. The upper half-inch of his forehead was several shades lighter than the rest of his tanned face because he always wore the same dirty cap when he was outside. In spite of that, his eyes were permanently wrinkled in a squint from years of looking out to sea for signs of fish.

He took his billed cap off his graying head and tossed it onto the straight-backed chair set beside the door.

The hat was so filthy you could hardly tell what color it was anymore. Since Mr. Wilson wouldn't allow his wife to do laundry on Sundays, and since he wore the hat from Monday to Saturday, she could never get it away from him to wash it.

Sara's mother glanced up from the eggs she was carefully turning and said, "Breakfast will be ready in a minute."

"Okay. I'll just wash up." Mr. Wilson proceeded on through the house while Ruth said to Joy, "Get Gram."

After breakfast Sara cleared away the unused food, washed and dried the dishes, and set about the task of making two apple pies. She turned on the radio and while she worked she engaged in her favorite occupation—daydreaming about the time some guy would discover she was a raving beauty. If she was going to dream, she might as well dream big! Mr. Wonderful would decide that she was the perfect girl for him. No others would ever do.

Measuring the flour and slicing and spicing the apples kept her body occupied, but allowed her mind to take off. She'd made so many of these pies she could probably make them in her sleep, she thought with a grimace. Once you learned how to do something in this family, you were stuck with that chore for the rest of your life.

She and her best friend, Susy Pitcher, used to sit in her room and talk about their idea of the perfect guy. The last time they'd done that, Sara had outlined her criteria. He had to be tall, at least six feet. And she was partial to dark brown hair, maybe with auburn highlights like hers. She wanted a guy with lots of muscles, one who would make her feel protected and safe. Also, she'd always thought blue eyes, the color of the Atlantic Ocean when there was a storm brewing, would be great. And then Susy had delivered the shocker. She'd said,

"Hey, you just described Jeff to a tee. Why don't you go for him?"

Sara had sat there, mouth gaping open like a frog waiting for a fly. Jeff? He already had a girlfriend; he always did. They never lasted long, but there was usually someone at school he was going out with. Besides, he treated Sara like a sister, and that was easy to understand. Since the two families had known each other forever, it was only logical that he'd never seen her as dating material. No, Sara had said firmly, she'd have to shop around and find someone else. The trouble was, there weren't any guys in her class that made her lights turn on. They were okay, some were even a little more than okay, but, well . . . Sara sighed as she rolled pastry and gently laid it in the pie pan. I need somebody new, she thought.

She was just beginning to roll out the second crust when there was a lot of noise, voices laughing and doors slamming. She knew, even before Joy ran in to announce them, that the Moores had invaded the house. Her mother expected her to greet them like special guests even though they knew each other like the backs of their hands, so Sara quickly removed her apron and walked out to do her duty.

The first person she saw was Jeff. He was dressed in jeans that were fully as worn as Sara's, but somehow he looked good in his. He had on a plaid flannel shirt in rust and navy that went really well with his tanned face and hands. Since he spent almost every weekend out on the boat, he was tanned even in winter.

As she came through the door, Jeff looked over at her. Sara thought she saw something in his expression she couldn't quite figure out; then it was gone. Probably he was just hungry, she told herself in a private joke. It was no secret that when the Moore boys came for dinner they ate as though they weren't fed regularly at home. Jim Moore claimed it was because no one cooked like Ruth Wilson. Sara thought that was a nasty thing to say in front of his wife. But Doris Moore always agreed, beaming widely. Maybe, unlike most of the other wives Sara knew, Doris didn't think of cooking as being one of the most important functions of being a fisherman's wife.

Everyone started greeting everyone else, seemingly at the top of their lungs and at the same time.

"Hiya, Sara," Jim Moore boomed. "Just as pretty as ever, I see."

Sara smiled weakly and managed a thank-you, which she knew no one heard. The way Mr. Moore talked about how pretty she was used to embarrass her, especially since she didn't agree. But she had decided he complimented her as a way of greeting her and didn't really mean it anyway.

"You boys come back here!" Doris yelled uselessly as her two youngest children scrambled up the stairs on Joy's heels.

"Keep out of my stuff," Sara called after the trio, knowing she was wasting her breath.

"Hey, Jim, will the fish ever run again?" Mr. Wilson asked his guest.

Sara was glad she had pies to make. She turned to escape in the direction of the kitchen and was stopped by Jeff's voice.

"Hey, Sara, want to play backgammon?"

She tried not to look at him bug-eyed. That was Gram's bit—making suggestions on how she and Jeff could spend time together.

"Sure, but I have to finish making some pies first."

"That's okay. We can play in the kitchen. I'll get the game and join you."

"All right." Sara struggled to keep her voice natural,

then turned and went back to the kitchen to continue rolling out the last crust.

When Jeff came into the room he was carrying the fancy backgammon game Sara kept hidden high up in her closet. "I just wanted to beat Gram to it this time," he told her with a grin.

Sara was surprised he didn't sound particularly bothered by Gram's trying to throw them together all the time.

He set the game on the table and opened it. "The guys are okay, so far," he reported.

Sara knew he must have checked on them while he was up there getting the game. She never thought it weird that he was almost as familiar with her room as he was with his own. When two families acted like they were extensions of each other, it wasn't surprising that each knew a lot about how the other lived.

"Oh? What're they doing?"

"Well, right now Robbie is drawing a picture for Joy . . ."

"Hmmm," Sara grunted, concentrating on her pie.

". . . and Stewie is reading this best-seller called *My Secret Diary*," Jeff continued with a twinkle in his eye.

The rolling pin hit the table with a loud thump. "My diary!" Sara exclaimed, her hand to her mouth.

"Just kidding!" Jeff said hastily as Sara started to rush out of the kitchen. "I saw it all safe and sound up in your closet when I got the game."

"You rat!" Sara sputtered, and threw a handful of flour at him. She loved it when Jeff teased her, but she'd rather die than let him know it.

He laughed and ducked. "Temper, temper!"

The flour was all over the floor, the table, and Jeff's chair. While Sara cleaned it up, Jeff calmly began setting up the game. When she was done she placed the top crust on the second pie, crimped it with the special pattern she liked to make, and covered the edges of both pies with damp cloths to prevent them from overbrowning in the oven. She popped the pies in the oven, set the timer, and washed her hands before removing the floury apron.

As she sat down opposite Jeff, he asked, "Brown or white pieces?"

"White. It always reminds me of Fannie Farmer white chocolate," Sara said.

Jeff picked up one of the playing pieces, bit it, and said, "Nope. Divinity fudge."

Sara giggled.

He shifted the game so the side with the white pieces already set up was on her side of the table and they began playing. A toss of the die made Jeff the first to play. Five turns later he sent one of her pieces to the middle.

"You rat!" Sara scolded in mock anger. "Just for that, I declare war!"

On her next turn she got off the bar and zapped one of Jeff's pieces and it was his turn to be on the bar. Sara laughed and kidded him about it.

Suddenly the timer went off and Sara checked the pies. Removing the wet rags, she reset the timer to tell her when they would be finally done, and returned to the game.

Two turns later Jeff started sending his pieces home while she was still trying to get all hers together to do the same thing. Then he said something that completely blew her concentration on the game.

"Got any plans for Friday night?" he asked offhandedly.

Everything stopped for Sara. Why had he asked that? Did they need her to baby-sit Robbie and Stewie? Help! Please let it not be that.

"Uh, why?" she asked carefully.

Jeff raised his head, looking at her oddly. "Well, I thought we might go to a movie. Maybe go for a pizza afterward. How about it?"

If it was possible for blood to stop in a person's veins, that was what happened to Sara. It took fully thirty seconds for her muddled brain to realize that Jeff Moore had just asked her for a date!

"Well?" For the first time Jeff smiled, as if her stunned silence was funny. She felt like a total fool.

"Yes. I would." Her tongue tripped over itself in her haste to answer.

"Good," he said with a grin, then rolled his die and took his last two pieces home. "I won."

"Rats!" Sara tried to sound disappointed, but didn't really care.

"Another game?" he asked.

"Sure."

Jeff began setting the board up, and the timer went off again. Sara rose to remove the pies from the oven. She set them to cool on wire racks, then came back to the table.

Jeff inhaled deeply. "Mmmm, apple pie! My favorite."

"You Moore boys like *every* pie, especially if it's made by a Wilson!" Sara scolded, but secretly she was glad she'd made apple pie. She told herself it was because it was nice to be appreciated, not because apple was Jeff's favorite.

They began playing the second game, but Sara found she couldn't concentrate on it. Her thoughts were racing ahead to Friday night. Wait until Susy heard! She'd never believe it! Jeff Moore asking Sara out. She turned over in her mind all her options of what to wear. Jeans? A skirt? Dress slacks? Maybe she could get her mom to let her buy something new.

Her mom! Sara hadn't asked her parents if she could go out with Jeff on Friday and she'd already told him yes. Surely they wouldn't object—especially since it was Jeff who wanted to take her out. But still, her father expected her to ask and she always had in the past. Well, she'd just have to take the chance that her father would agree.

Jeff pounced on one of her pieces, sending her to the bar again.

"Hey! You creep!" she objected. That would teach her to daydream and not pay attention to the game.

She devoted herself to the game with a vengeance and sent Jeff to the bar twice. By jealously guarding her pieces, she sent all of them home. "I won!" she cried smugly. "See? You've been punished for playing dirty."

Jeff just grinned. "Okay. Now we have to play a third game to break the tie."

"Yeah," Sara agreed, getting an idea. "You set it up. I have to check with Mom about something." She stood and hurried out to the living room.

Mrs. Wilson was deep in conversation with Doris and Sara hated to interrupt her. She didn't want anyone else to hear her ask about going out with Jeff. She was afraid they'd make a big deal out of it and then Jeff would know she'd had to ask for permission. A sixteen-year-old asking permission to go out on a date! It was one of her father's rules that bugged her.

She managed to get her mother's attention, got her to come with her into the hall, and quickly and quietly told her about Jeff's asking her out.

"Why, isn't that great," Mrs. Wilson said softly. "I'm sure your father won't object." She glanced in at the others gathered in the living room, then back at Sara. Smiling, she said, "I'll ask him after everyone leaves. Is that soon enough?"

"Yes." It would have to be. Sara knew that if her mother asked her father right away, then everyone would hear about it.

She returned to the kitchen, where Jeff was patiently waiting. He trounced her at backgammon, but she didn't care. Any guy who was going to take her out to a movie and for pizza deserved to win two games out of three. She wouldn't even let herself think about the possibility that her father would say no. He just had to say yes!

Just as Jeff and Sara were folding up the game, their mothers came out into the kitchen to start dinner preparations. Sara had to help them, but Jeff got shooed from the room.

"Can't have any men underfoot," Sara's mother teased.

Sara watched him go with a trace of sadness. In this house there was a definite line between men's work and women's work, and nobody crossed it. It was different in Jeff's house. He helped out from time to time, and some of the best memories Sara had were of her and Jeff fooling around in his kitchen.

Finally everyone was seated in the dining room at the huge oak table, made larger by the addition of two extra leaves. The aroma of baked ham mingled with the smell of sweet potatoes, green beans, and hot biscuits. Everyone was talking at once as usual. Robbie and Stewie were arguing over something; Joy was tattling to Doris about what they'd done to her room; the men were discussing sports; and Gram was telling Mrs. Wilson about the way she used to fix sweet-potato pie.

Sara noted that the only two not adding to the general din were herself and Jeff. She watched him as he passed the big bowls heaped with potatoes and beans, and the huge platter of ham. How strong his hands were, she thought. They were large and muscular from fishing, and she wondered if they were callused yet like her father's were. Jeff had awfully wide shoulders, too, that were strong from hauling in nets. She liked the way his eyes crinkled as he laughed at something Joy said.

Then she caught herself. How come she was noticing

things about Jeff as if this were the first time she'd ever seen him? It was as though, just because he'd asked her out for a date, that made things different. That was silly!

And why had he asked her out anyway? She tried to recall if he'd been dating anyone special lately. She seemed to remember he'd been going out with a girl who didn't live on the island, Leslie somebody. Sara didn't know her last name because, like Jeff, Leslie was a junior instead of a sophomore like Sara. Had Jeff had a fight with Leslie? Was that why he was asking Sara out—to get back at Leslie or make her jealous? Sara didn't think so; she was sure Jeff was too mature to act so childishly. So why ask *her* out?

# 2

She hadn't come up with any good explanation by the time the Moores left. As they all made their good-byes, Jeff didn't say anything about their date either. For one horrible moment Sara was afraid he'd forgotten he'd even asked, but then she realized he probably didn't want to talk about it in front of everyone else, too. She didn't know what time they'd be going out on Friday, but Jeff would tell her before then. She hoped!

After the door closed, Sara went off to get Joy ready for bed. She could hear her parents' voices in the living room and knew her mom was telling her dad about the date. Sara's heart stayed in her throat right up until Mrs. Wilson climbed the stairs to tell her it was okay. Then she sagged with relief and ran to the phone to call Susy.

"Wow!" Susy exclaimed when Sara told her. "Jeff

Moore. I can't believe it! Oh, Sara, you're so lucky."
A slightly envious tone crept into Susy's voice. Sara knew
Susy had had a crush on Jeff a long time ago, and even
though she claimed she didn't anymore, Sara thought
secretly that Susy still did. She'd seen Susy's eyes following Jeff whenever they were all gathered at the bus stop,
although he never treated Susy any differently than he
did all the other girls. But then, he'd never really treated
her, Sara, any differently either. Until today. . . .

"So what do you think?" Susy's words dragged Sara's
thoughts back to the present.

"About what?" she was forced to ask.

Susy sounded a little annoyed as she repeated, "I
asked what makes you special enough for him to ask
you out? I mean, you know, he never asked you out
before."

That was exactly what Sara had been asking herself.
What was special about her besides the fact that her
family and Jeff's had been close friends for years? Sara
couldn't think of a thing. "I don't know," she answered
truthfully.

"Well, there's gotta be some reason," Susy said after
a pause. Then she added a little wistfully, "I wish it
was me going out Friday. I mean . . . I wish we *both*
had a date."

The girls talked a little longer and then Sara had to
go get ready for bed herself. Her father was adamant
about her getting to bed by nine o'clock on nights before
school. Susy was able to stay up until ten. Sara was a
little jealous of her for that.

As she lay in the dark listening to Joy's deep breathing
and the constant patter of rain on the roof, she thought
how it had turned out to be a beautiful day after all—
in spite of the weather! But her happiness was marred
a little when she thought about Susy's question. What
made her special enough for Jeff to ask her out? Looks?
No! Popularity? Certainly not!

She snuggled down under the quilt and sighed. She'd just have to wait and see, she decided, and the next thing she knew, it was morning.

Monday dawned bright and sunny—the perfect match for Sara's mood as she stood waiting on the road for Susy to catch up with her. They walked to the bus stop together every morning, and today the main topic of discussion was Jeff. They switched to science as soon as they got within hearing distance. He stood with two other guys who shared the bus stop.

Jeff hardly noticed them and Sara felt let down.

"You'd think if a guy asked you out, the least he could do was speak to you at the bus stop," she grumbled to Susy.

Susy looked at Jeff and then her attention was caught by something else. "Hey, look! There's a girl coming down the road. Do you think she's coming here?"

Sara glanced over her shoulder and saw a girl she didn't know walking slowly toward the cluster of kids. When she got ten feet away she came to a stop and turned toward the road. She began studying a piece of paper she pulled out of her leather shoulder bag. Sara thought she looked a little stuck-up.

"Get a load of that purse!" Susy exclaimed. "It must have cost fifty bucks."

Sara agreed, wondering where the girl had come from. She was really pretty, with dark blue eyes and red hair. Nature had been kind to her and hadn't given her any freckles on her face to go with the red hair. She had on tight, expensive designer jeans. She wore a short rose-colored bubble jacket and the kind of leather cowboy boots Sara had only seen in magazines. By comparison Sara felt like a dirt-poor country bumpkin in her plain serviceable jeans, ordinary wool jacket that she'd outgrown during the last year, and sneakers.

Stan Love, who'd made it his life's work to live up to his name, suddenly noticed the newcomer and jabbed

Jeff on the arm. The three guys stopped talking about basketball and started sizing up the girl. Sara thought she'd have died on the spot if they ever did that to her. The girl gave them a look that showed she considered them silly little boys and went back to studying her paper. By now she must have that thing memorized, Sara thought.

Carteret Island residents weren't necessarily unfriendly to strangers, they just took a while to warm up to one. The island kids didn't exactly stampede new ones, either. Sara watched the boys joking and snickering a little, then saw the girl give them a sideways look. A telltale pink colored her cheeks. Why, she's not as stuck-up as she looks, Sara realized, suddenly feeling sorry for her. If she were the new girl, she'd have hated it the way the five kids at the bus stop were keeping back.

"Let's go over and introduce ourselves," she suggested impulsively.

Susy glanced at the girl. "I don't know. She looks older than us. Besides, she could have come up to us instead of planting herself way over there."

Sara bit her lip. She didn't want to go over alone, and she didn't feel like pushing Susy. She glanced at her watch. The bus was due in about five minutes. Getting up her courage, she marched over to the trio of boys as if that were something she did all the time. They looked at her, and Jeff's expression was the only one that wasn't suspicious.

"I see you noticed her," she said with a nod at the girl.

"Yeah," the three murmured in unison.

Susy had trailed after her and Sara felt all four pairs of eyes staring at her.

"I . . . uh . . . was thinking . . ."

"Wow!" Stan Love snickered.

Sara glared at him and went on. "I'll bet she feels

bad, standing over there with no one making a move to be friendly."

"I'd be glad to make a move toward her," Stan drawled, making Pete Smith chuckle like a maniac.

Sara aimed another killing look at Stan, but it didn't shorten his life by even a second. She turned to Jeff.

"Yeah, you're probably right," he agreed, looking at the girl thoughtfully. He took Sara's arm and started walking toward the girl. "So let's go make like the welcome wagon."

Sara had only a couple of seconds to enjoy the feel of Jeff's hand on her arm and then they were standing in front of the girl. When she raised her head and saw them, her face broke into a smile.

She was even prettier when she smiled, Sara thought. She noticed Jeff seemed to be impressed with the girl's transformation, too, and a funny hollow feeling settled deep inside her.

"Hi," Jeff said. "I'm Jeff Moore, and this is Sara Wilson. I guess you're new?"

"Yeah. I'm Jackie Wells. My parents moved here last week but I didn't fly down till yesterday."

The minute she spoke, Sara knew she was from someplace other than the South. "Where are you from?" she asked.

"Long Island. You know, New York?"

"Yeah, sure, I know." Did Jackie think they didn't learn geography down here? Sara wondered, then told herself not to be so sensitive.

The other three had come over by now and Jeff introduced them, calling them "these unfriendly clods" and adding that if Jackie was smart she'd avoid Stan Love as if he were nuclear waste. "You know, like the Love canal?" he joked, to the groans of everyone else.

Jackie just laughed and said, "Hey, if I can handle New York wolves, I can handle country wolves."

Stan stood over her and leered. "Oh, yeah?"

"Down, boy," Jackie said in a bored tone, shooing him away like a bothersome fly.

Everyone laughed and started asking questions. They found out she was an only child and a junior. The piece of paper she'd been studying was her schedule, but she wanted something changed. Jeff offered to show her where Guidance was as soon as they got to school. Jackie gazed up into his eyes with obvious appreciation and said, "Hey, thanks."

Sara was proud that Jeff had taken the lead in the difficult business of meeting the new girl. The fact that he was equally friendly with everyone lent to his popularity. It made her all the more pleased that he was taking her out Friday.

The bus wheezed up the road and groaned to a stop. The six kids piled on and Sara headed for her usual seat, four rows back. Maybe now Jeff would sit with her and discuss their plans for Friday. To her disappointment Susy plopped down beside her like she always did and Jeff went on past to his spot in the back. Jackie sat in the back too, flanked by Pete and Stan, who clearly intended to let no grass grow under their feet around the new girl.

After the bus had rumbled forward, Susy shook her head. "Good grief! Jeff asks you out yesterday and today he's playing tour guide to the new girl. How many girls does he need?"

"Oh, come on, Susy. He's just being nice, that's all," Sara defended him automatically.

"Yeah, right. And I suppose Pete and Stan are just being nice, too?"

"Oh, that's different. They're . . ." Sara glanced back to see what the two boys were doing, and her face clouded. Jeff was leaning over Jackie's seat, and she was basking in the attention she was getting from the three guys. Sara turned around and frowned out the window.

"And did you get a load of that accent? What's the matter with people up north? Don't they know that if there's an R in a word, you're supposed to pronounce it? Sheesh! I mean, really." She began mimicking Jackie. "My parents moved he-uh last week . . ."

Sara tuned her out and pretended she had some last-minute homework to do so she wouldn't have to talk to Susy. But inside she was thinking. Jeff *was* just being nice, wasn't he? There wasn't anything else to it, was there? Sure Jackie was pretty, even if she did talk strangely. Prettier than Sara, for sure. Jeff hadn't been paying Sara too much attention at the bus stop, and he hadn't actually spoken to her at all once they went over to meet Jackie. She remembered he'd dropped her arm as soon as they'd gotten there. Actually, Jackie had stolen the show completely after that.

Stop it! Sara scolded herself. This was ridiculous. She was just jealous of the attention Jeff gave Jackie when she'd been hoping he'd talk to her about their date. So what if he didn't? He'd get around to it. She didn't own him. And she was the one who had started the whole thing off about Jackie. Sara shook her head at her own childishness and turned to talk to Susy about their upcoming algebra exam.

When the bus finally reached the school forty minutes later, Sara got off and stood waiting for Jackie. If Jeff could be friendly, so could she. She'd just wish her good luck on her first day of school, that's all, and if Jeff wanted to casually mention their date, that would be great.

Jackie stepped off the bus with her three-man combo on her trail.

"Good luck on your first day," Sara said sincerely.

Jackie smiled. "Thanks, but I don't think I'm going to need it now." She looked back at Jeff, who took her arm the same way he'd taken Sara's.

"Come on, I'll show you where Guidance is, then I'll have to beat feet for class."

"Great." Jackie turned toward the school and exclaimed, "Hey! This isn't as bad as I expected."

"What'd you expect? The little red schoolhouse on the prairie?" Jeff wisecracked. "We even have indoor plumbing."

Jackie laughed and Jeff hurried her away, leaving Sara in a pool of misery. She watched Jeff disappear into the crowd. It would have been nice if he'd at least said "good-bye" or "see you later." But he'd never done that before, so why should he start now? Just because they were going out on a date Friday? Sara shook her head and followed Susy, who'd already headed for the main door. What a dope you are, Sara. One date that hasn't even happened yet does not make us a steady couple. He's free to do what he wants. With this pep talk Sara marched into school, her head high.

Throughout the day Sara had to repeat those words to herself. Especially when she saw Jeff and Jackie at lunch. It looked like he'd appointed himself her personal guide. He took her to his table and introduced her to the other juniors sitting there. As Jackie passed the table next to Sara's, one guy pointed her out to another.

"There's the girl I told you about. I mean, has she got a bod or what?"

"For sure!"

Sara lost interest in her food after overhearing this. She knew her own figure was adequate; by no stretch of the imagination could she be called flat-chested. But she'd never give Dolly Parton a run for her money either.

When everyone got back on the bus at the end of the day, Sara saw with intense relief that Jackie had made friends with one of the girls from another bus stop and sat with her. Jeff joined his friends in the back with nothing more than a brief greeting to Jackie.

Sara smiled to herself. See? What were you so uptight about?

"Want to come home with me after school and help me decide what to wear Friday?" she asked Susy.

"Sure."

After the girls greeted Mrs. Wilson and sampled some of her applesauce cake, they retreated to Sara's room and started going through her wardrobe. They pulled out all of her slacks, blouses, sweaters, and skirts, mixing and matching them until all the possibilities were exhausted, but no matter what Sara decided on, Susy always seemed to have an argument against it.

"You don't want that skirt. What if everyone's in jeans?"

Then when Sara picked up a pair of her best jeans to match with a sweater, Susy said, "Gosh. It's too bad you don't have jeans like Jackie had on today."

Pretty soon Sara hated all her clothes and put everything away without settling on one outfit. "I'll do it later," she said. "I've got a lot of homework tonight anyway."

Her hint was taken and Susy left. Sometimes Susy could get on your nerves, Sara reflected as she gazed out the window over her desk. It would be nice to have a friend who didn't leave you feeling exhausted.

Sara shook her head and started on her homework. The room was dead quiet because Joy was told to stay out of it until after dinner each night to give Sara a place to study uninterrupted. But Sara's study kept being interrupted anyway—by thoughts of Jeff. Why hadn't he spoken to her yet about when he'd come for her Friday? Then she had the answer. They were going to the movies, right? And the movie started the same time every week. Subtract forty-five minutes to get there and you had the time Jeff would probably come. What a jerk she'd been! Jeff no doubt expected her to figure that out for herself. The fact that it took her over twenty-four hours to do it didn't put her in the genius class! But maybe she'd just been too preoccupied with the fact that he'd asked her out at all. Which brought her back to that same question. Why *had* he?

She'd been doodling and her doodles reminded her that her homework wasn't getting done. She'd just have to wait till Friday and hope Jeff said something that would give her a clue.

When Friday finally rolled around, Sara was a basket case. She actually walked out the door for the bus that morning and forgot to take her schoolbooks. Fortunately, before she'd gotten twenty feet from the house, her mother called after her. Sara's face flamed as she took the books; her mother's face had a humorous expression on it but she didn't say anything, for which Sara was grateful.

In math class the only equation she could think about was $1 + 1 = 2$. Sara plus Jeff equals . . . Then the teacher asked her a question and she said dreamily, "One plus one equals two." The whole class broke up and she wanted to drop through the floor.

At lunch she found she'd carried her tray halfway down the cafeteria line without taking anything and had to go back. Naturally she needed to cut in front of one of the guys from math class, who mimicked, "One plus one equals two, huh?"

She decided on the spot she was too excited to eat their "mystery-meat sandwich" or "guess-what parmesan with shoe strings." So she grabbed only a container of milk and fled to her table. Then of course during biology class, while there was a surprise quiz and the room was in perfect silence, her stomach started growling so loudly everyone within a five-foot radius could hear her.

She was never so glad to get on the bus to head home. But when Susy asked her what time Jeff was picking her up, she was reminded that he still hadn't said a thing to her about it. What if he'd forgotten he'd even asked her out? What if she got all dressed up and then sat downstairs waiting all night and he never showed up? She'd simply die!

"Forty-five minutes before the movie starts, of course," she said flippantly, and then sat there the rest of the ride to the island rehearsing in her mind this terrible scene where she sat in the living room for hours with three adults surrounding her, trying to be sympathetic, and making excuses why Jeff was late.

Susy led the way off the bus, and when she turned to talk to Sara, she looked over Sara's shoulder and said, "Uh, well, I'll be going now. I have to help Mom with some stuff after school," and she turned away, walking off.

Sara opened her mouth to call her, saw Jeff move up beside her, and shut her mouth.

Jeff said, "You still want to go to the movie tonight?"

Did she! "Yes," she said in a voice calmer than she thought possible.

"Okay. I'll be by at six-thirty."

All Sara could do was nod; her voice had disappeared someplace. No doubt engulfed by the balloon of happiness that was rising up inside.

Jeff started talking about a new boat his father wanted but wasn't sure he could afford, while Sara walked about ten feet off the ground and tried to pay attention. It wasn't easy. It was only when he said, "See you later," and headed for his house that she came back to earth.

"Yeah," she got out almost too late, and skipped home.

She hadn't felt this way about a date since her very first one last year. What made this so special? she asked herself as she pushed open the front door. Because it was with Jeff?

Gram was in the living room reading to Joy, and her mom was in the kitchen. Sara could tell by the aroma of fresh-baked bread. Monday was washday. Friday was bread day. And date day! After putting her books on the bottom step of the stairs leading up to her room, she floated into the kitchen.

Mrs. Wilson handed her a freshly sliced hunk of whole-wheat bread slathered with butter, the way Sara liked it, and poured water from the kettle into a cup. She placed an herbal tea bag in it and handed it to her daughter. Her eyes twinkled as she asked, "Have a good day in school?"

Sara nodded but decided against recounting all her mishaps. That would reveal how special this date was, and she wasn't ready for anyone—not even her mom—to know that. Instead she said her day was okay and that Jeff would be by for her around six-thirty.

"Then you can have the night off from kitchen duty to get yourself ready," Mrs. Wilson said kindly.

"Thanks, Mom!" Sara went upstairs to try to get some of her homework out of the way but ended up daydreaming until supper.

After the meal was over at five-thirty, she ran upstairs to shower and dress. There was the problem—what to wear? She dragged half a dozen outfits from her closet and tried them on.

"Oh, I can't stand any of them!" she said to the mirror just as Joy came in the room.

Joy watched her try on two more outfits and then asked, "What are you doing? Playing dress-up?"

Sara laughed and patted her sister's head fondly. "No, silly, going out on a date." Just the sound of the words gave Sara a rush of excitement.

Joy settled herself on Sara's bed amid the discarded clothes. "What's a date?"

Sara pulled off a sweater and without thinking tossed it in the direction of her bed. It hit Joy in the face. The little girl thought it was a game. She laughed, pulled it off her head, and threw it back at Sara. Sara walked over and placed it on her bed.

"It's when a guy and a girl go out to do something together," she explained.

"Like what?" Joy persisted, wiggling into the rejected sweater. The arms hung down past her hands by a foot.

"Oh . . . like a movie," Sara said vaguely, thinking: Wouldn't her folks be shocked if they knew what some other kids did on dates!

"Is that what you're going to do?" Joy's inquisitive voice broke in on her thoughts.

Sara's face flushed scarlet before she realized her sister had no idea what she'd just been thinking. "Uh, what?" she asked, picking up an almost sheer blouse and discarding it just as quickly.

"Going to a movie?"

"Yeah." Sara's voice was developing a slight edge. She had only thirty-five minutes before Jeff came and still she didn't have the slightest idea what to wear. And now Joy was starting to put on one of her skirts that she hadn't entirely decided against. She was going to have to get Joy out from under foot.

"Why don't you go see if Gram wants you?" she suggested.

"She's taking a nap."

"Oh. Then why don't you go talk to Daddy?"

"I can't. He went out."

Sara felt like screaming, but she forced herself to be patient. "Well, go see if Mom needs you." Her voice was reedy. If she didn't get Joy out of here, she'd never be ready on time.

"She doesn't," Joy informed her matter-of-factly. She stepped into a pair of Sara's heels and promptly fell over.

"How do you know?" Sara asked in exasperation, and reached to pull her sweater over Joy's head. Her hands stilled in midair when Joy said, " 'Cause she's in the living room talking to Jeff."

"Jeff!" Sara all but shrieked. Her watch said six-oh-five. He was twenty-five minutes early and she still wasn't dressed!

Frantically she dived into the reject pile for a pair of plum-colored corduroy jeans and yanked them on. She stepped into a pair of beige ankle boots and pulled on a fisherman's knit sweater Gram had made. She always got compliments when she wore it.

As she ran down the hall to the bathroom, Sara fastened a gold heart-shaped locket on a chain around her neck. The heart was empty because she'd never been able to figure out whose picture she should put in it. That's just like me, she thought as she stopped to clasp the chain. My heart is empty and I never know who to put in it. Would Jeff be the one?

Joy followed Sara into the bathroom, tagging on her heels as if she were connected to Sara by a rope. Sara dumped her makeup on the bathroom counter and started putting pale lilac eye shadow on. She got it too heavy and had to remove some with a cotton ball. A little gray eye shadow made the color less obvious, more natural. Then she picked up her mascara. Her hand shook so badly she had to clamp her elbow with the other hand. Joy moved into position to watch her sister more closely.

"Joy, you know you're not supposed to stand on the toilet," Sara scolded, taking her eyes off the image in the mirror to look at Joy. When she turned back she accidentally stabbed herself in the eyeball. "Ow!" Both eyes started running, and the black mascara mixed with tears to form two dripping rings around her eyes. "Look what you made me do!" Sara accused Joy. "Now I've got two black eyes."

"You look like a raccoon!" Joy chortled.

Sara found no humor in the remark. She grabbed a tissue, cleaned off most of the mess, and finished doing her mascara without mishap.

Then she reached for her lipstick, and just as she went to outline her mouth, she heard Jeff's deep-timbre laughter booming from the living room. Her heart leapt, her hand jerked, and she looked like a clown with huge lips.

"O-o-o-o-h!" She scrubbed the lipstick off and redid it.

Joy was laughing so hard she collapsed on the bathroom rug. Sara used one foot to nudge her out the way while she managed to get her hair brushed with about five strokes. Then she scurried back into her room to grab up her purse.

She headed for the top of the stairs and stopped to catch her breath. Joy, who'd been close on her heels, plowed into her. After disentangling the five-year-old, Sara took a deep breath and slowly and deliberately started down the stairs as if she had all the time in the world.

Joy's voice rose in the clear, high pitch of a confused preschooler. "How come you rushed around upstairs and now you're walking real slow?"

Sara turned on her like a hawk swooping on its prey. "Shhh!"

Joy's head jerked back as if she'd been slugged. Sara felt momentary remorse and then continued her walk down the stairs, saying to herself as a foot touched each step: "Act casual . . . act casual . . . act casual . . ."

She entered the living room and exclaimed, "Oh, Jeff! You're here already?" She'd done it! The perfect degree of surprise in her voice.

"But I told you up—" Joy's mouth snapped shut as Sara grabbed her shoulder and ushered her out into the hall.

"Joy, I left my coat upstairs. Will you get it, please?"

Sara asked in a loud voice. Then she bent down with her mouth against Joy's ear and whispered fiercely, "And don't you *dare* say a thing about telling me Jeff was here!"

Joy looked both frightened and puzzled. Sara could hear her muttering as she plodded back up the stairs on her short legs. "Boy, big sisters are weird . . ." Her voice trailed off as she reached the landing and turned toward their bedroom.

Sara felt about two inches tall. She really shouldn't have been so rough on her little sister. But Joy had such a big mouth! Sara turned toward the living room, trying to stand up a little taller, and walked back in.

This time she noticed Jeff's clothes—nice but not dressy. His jeans looked new, and he had on a ski sweater in a combination of browns. His favorite pair of tooled leather boots, polished to a gleam, showed beneath the hem of his pants. He was casual and neat, but it was clear to Sara that he hadn't taken any special pains to dress up. And she'd spent literally days fussing over what to wear! Well, what had she really expected? She was just Old Sara, the family friend. Why get all fancy for her? Feeling a little let down, she forced herself to smile, but she felt awkward. She was saved from saying anything by Joy's half-stomping, half-walking back down the stairs with Sara's short jacket slung over her arm. Before the little girl could say something incriminating, Sara took the coat, said, "Thanks," and hastily headed for the door.

"Guess we ought to get going, Jeff. We've got a forty-five-minute drive ahead of us."

"Uh, yeah." Jeff looked a little taken aback by her apparent impatience to get out of the house, but he joined her at the front door. " 'Bye, Mrs. Wilson. 'Bye, Joy."

" 'Bye, Jeff, Sara. Have a good time." Mrs. Wilson beamed at them as Sara, in an uncharacteristic move, took Jeff by the arm and pulled him out the door.

Joy stood in the open doorway, watching them go with an expression on her face that showed she thought her sister had cracked up.

"That Joy sure is cute," Jeff commented as he held the door to his pickup open for Sara.

"Yeah," Sara agreed, but added silently: When she keeps her mouth shut!

# 3

Once they were on their way, Sara found to her horror that she was afflicted with the condition she'd wished on her sister—the cat had her tongue. She sat there like a piece of dead wood on her half of the seat, searching frantically for something to say. It wasn't as if she were in strange surroundings. She'd ridden in this truck lots of times before with Jeff. They had to run errands once in a while, although usually one of Jeff's brothers was with them. Everything was familiar—the faint smell of oil the cab always had, even the vague aroma of fish from all the times Jeff had carted nets or other gear. And yet, everything was different. She and Jeff were not on an errand, but a date.

Jeff pulled onto the bridge that connected Carteret Island with the mainland and glanced at Sara. "I didn't see your pop or Shep around tonight."

"Yeah. You know how Carl Bradley just got out of the hospital? He's not supposed to lift a finger around his house. I think Dad went over there to see if he could help Carl out with something, and naturally he just has to take that dog with him." Sara laughed. "Those two are inseparable."

"I know what you mean. That's the way Dad was before his dog died." Jeff smiled and looked forward.

Sara was struck with how handsome his profile was. Why hadn't she ever noticed how really good-looking he was? Or maybe she'd simply accepted it and ignored it since he was just an old friend. Good grief, they'd known each other since they were in diapers.

And what had she been doing while Jeff grew into a handsome seventeen-year-old? Just being the same old fat-cheeked Sara! She stifled a sigh of disgust.

Jeff was talking about school and the tons of homework he'd been getting lately. Sara switched from being self-pitying to attentive.

"Chemistry's not hard; it's just a pain in the neck. My dad once asked what a guy who was going to be a fisherman needed with chemistry, and even I had a hard time explaining," Jeff was saying.

They got involved in a conversation about just what kind of an occupation would demand chemistry as a prerequisite and the forty-five-minute drive to Morehead City flew by.

Jeff parked the truck and they headed for the theater. A gust of cold wind blew in their faces as they rounded a corner.

"Nippy," Jeff commented. "You warm enough?"

"Yeah." Sara wondered if she'd said no, if he'd have put his arm around her. For Pete's sake! She was getting ridiculously romantic about a first date! One thing was for sure, she'd better develop a more lively personality or this would definitely be their last.

As they stood in line for the tickets, Sara glanced around, spotting several kids she knew. A girl from her math class smiled at her, reminding her of the "one-plus-one" fiasco. Could the girl now guess what Sara had been thinking about, seeing her with Jeff?

She looked away. Her gaze stopped on another girl—the one Jeff had last been dating. Leslie's brown eyes opened in surprise as she did a double-take. It looked like she couldn't believe Sara was with Jeff. Then a smirk twisted her mouth and she turned away, her nose in the air, and entwined her arm in the boy's next to her.

Jeff, who now had the tickets, lightly touched Sara's shoulder. "Want popcorn?" he asked.

"Okay." Sara followed him over to the refreshment stand, and then each carried a container of popcorn into the theater. Some of the joy of being out with Jeff faded away. It was pretty clear that Leslie still had a thing for Jeff and didn't consider Sara a threat. Had she and Jeff had a fight? If Jeff had asked Sara out to make Leslie mad, he'd failed.

"Where do you want to sit?" Jeff paused halfway down the aisle.

"Oh, here's okay." At least a mile away from Leslie!

"Then pick a seat."

Sara slid into the middle of the row, as another couple entered the row in front of them from the opposite side of the theater.

"Hey, Jeff." The boy lifted his popcorn container in greeting.

"Hi, Mike. I suppose this movie is part of your research for that social-studies assignment?" Jeff grinned.

"Of course! I'm doing a paper on the effect of James Bond on the social consciousness of the American teen-ager." Mike looked like he was perfectly serious, but the girl with him burst out laughing.

"Oh, sure, Mike. That should earn you at least a fifty-five!"

Sara recognized the girl from school. Her name was Peg Bennett and she and Mike were both juniors. Peg smiled at Sara and said, "Hi."

"Hi. He isn't serious, is he?" Sara asked, and then felt dumb when the other three laughed.

"No," Peg said. "You'll just have to get used to his sense of humor. It's as warped as his mind."

Mike put on an insulted look. "Oh, yeah? That says a lot for your taste in men."

"Don't let my going out with you go to your head," Peg shot back. "I'm just waiting for Mr. Perfect to come along and then it'll be bye-bye Mike-e-e-e."

Sara looked at Jeff, who smiled, leaned close, and said, "Don't pay any attention to them. They're nuts about each other." Then he started throwing popcorn up in the air and trying to catch it with his mouth. He caught one and then nudged Mike. "Hey, Mike, I bet you can't beat me in the popcorn toss."

"Ha! Stand back, you amateur, and watch a pro in action."

The two guys started throwing popcorn up in the air as fast as they could and catching it in their mouths.

Peg turned back to Sara. "Do you believe these guys?"

"No." Sara laughed. "They aren't even chewing. What are they doing, swallowing it whole?"

Mike took time out to explain. "No, we're storing it in our cheeks like chipmunks." He puffed out his face in illustration.

Sara started laughing. She was grateful all the nonsense made it unnecessary for her to have to talk to Jeff. Her mind still seemed to have a blank tape in it and she couldn't think of anything to do but eat her popcorn.

Jeff and Mike continued the kernel-toss competition, while Sara and Peg kept track of how many they successfully caught. Some of the other guys in the audience noticed what they were doing and joined the contest. Soon guys all over the theater were littering the place with missed popcorn.

"Look what you idiots started," Peg scolded. "The manager is going to throw us all out of here."

"No, he won't. He needs the profits too much," Jeff argued, and went to toss another piece in the air, but it went wild. Sara felt something land in her hair. "Oops! Sorry." Jeff reached out to retrieve the runaway kernel. It had lodged in the curls she'd made in the sides of her hair with her blow dryer.

She felt his fingers combing out her curl, and a tingling sensation ran over her skin. She tried to keep still, and had to resist the urge to lean toward him so his hand would stay in her hair. What was happening to her? She'd been held by guys on the dance floor and not cared. But this was so different.

The lights dimmed and the kids began cheering. Wolf calls accompanied the credits. Jeff leaned over to talk to Mike.

"Okay, professor, explain why James Bond movies always start with gorgeous women cavorting on the screen as the credits roll by."

"Elementary, my dear Watson. To give people in the audience ideas." He leaned toward Peg, threw his arm around her, and said in a thick French accent, "Geeve us a kees."

Peg pushed him back. "Give *me* a break. And what's with the 'us'? Am I supposed to pucker up for the whole crowd?"

A guy in the row in front of them turned around with a grin. "Hey, yeah, that sounds good. Me first."

"Oh, no you don't." Mike rose to the bait.

Someone in back hissed at them. "Shhhh!"

The movie began and for a while Sara concentrated on the action, but then a different kind of action took her attention. Jeff was so tall, his legs were cramped in the row. His knee kept touching Sara's. At first she held herself rigid to keep from relaxing against him. But he was so big, the only way to break contact permanently would be to sit two seats away. What a jerk I'm being! she thought. Jeff shifted in the seat as if he were growing larger by the minute, and his shoulder nudged hers. She peeked at his face but he seemed engrossed in the movie. She was the only one who seemed to notice the cramped quarters, and she was overreacting.

She settled down and tried to relax. But she couldn't help thinking about what would happen after the show. Would he kiss her when he took her home? Maybe soon he'd take her hand in his and hold it through the rest of the movie. . . .

Suddenly Sara came to her senses. What was the matter with her? She was making a big deal out of a simple movie date! If she didn't stop thinking this way, soon she'd have them married and settled down with kids! It wasn't like her to get carried away with silly dreams. She was more practical. Her father always called her "sensible Sara." So why couldn't she be sensible right now?

Jeff moved again and this time he laid his arm along the back of her seat. That did it! Her imagination moved into high gear. She wondered if putting his arm along the back of her seat was the prelude to putting it around her. But the sensible part of her said: Guys were always wiggly. They had so much energy they didn't know what to do with it.

Unfortunately—or fortunately, Sara wasn't sure—nothing happened. A few minutes later Jeff moved again and put his other arm along the back of the empty seat

next to him and withdrew the one behind Sara. He left
it that way the rest of the movie. She felt deserted somehow.

When the lights came back on, Mike turned toward
them. "You guys want to join us at the Pizza Inn?"

Jeff looked at Sara, who nodded. If there was any way
this date could last longer, she was up for it.

"Sure, why not?" he said with a shrug.

The four of them made their way out of the theater
and proceeded to the pizza place. Already it was filling
up with the movie crowd. Mike grabbed one of the last
booths and they all slid in, the girls on the inside, the
guys on the outside, where their long legs could fight
over the space in the aisle. When they were seated with
their coats off, Peg and Sara decided they needed to
go check their makeup in the ladies' room. The guys
let them out with a lot of good-natured complaining.
When they came back, a lively discussion began about
what kind of pizza to order.

"I don't want any of those little fishies on mine," Mike
informed them in a falsetto voice.

"Traitor!" Sara scolded in a deep voice.

"Yeah, Mike," Peg added. "The least you could do
is eat a fish or two for the local economy."

"But they don't catch anchovies around here!" Mike
protested.

"No?" Sara feigned surprise, and then smiled pertly
across the table. "Well, then, I guess you're off the *hook*,
Mike."

"Booo," everyone chorused.

They ordered a large pepperoni-and-mushroom pizza
and Cokes. A few kids they knew spoke to them as they
passed by. When they'd moved on, Jeff asked, "How
much do you think we'll beat Topsail by this next game?"

Topsail was the team the Carteret High Mariners had
to play next in basketball.

"One hundred to zero," Mike pronounced; then, mimicking Howard Cosell, he added, "They are so bad, the coach has to explain how to play the game to them every time."

"Not only that," Sara added, "they even forget what a basketball is. The coach has to show it to them in the locker room right before each game."

"Uh, here's your basic basketball, fellas. Note that it is r-o-u-n-d," Mike intoned in the voice of somebody with an IQ of fifty.

Peg and Sara giggled, but Jeff just smiled. Apparently he didn't find it as funny as they did, maybe because he had to take the subject seriously. He was sportswriter for the school paper. "I've been watching Topsail, and you just might have to eat your words. They'll probably beat us, and then you won't have anything to laugh about."

"The voice of doom," Mike mocked, smiling. "That's the trouble with having a sportswriter in your midst. He's always a wet blanket."

Their pizza was delivered to the table and they started fighting over the biggest piece and the one with the most pepperoni.

"I should have it," Mike said. "I'm still a growing boy."

"That's for sure," Peg said, patting his stomach.

"No, I should have it because I'm the smallest and I need to catch up with the rest of you," Sara argued.

"Age before youth. I should have it," Peg said, trying to look old and in need of sustenance.

"Then I should have it because I'm the youngest. *Old* people should eat less, my Gram says," Sara insisted.

Mike calmly reached out and took the piece under discussion. Now it was his turn to get booed. Sara swooped in with her fork and stole a piece of pepperoni from his piece.

"Hey!" Jeff turned to her with a startled expression.

The laughter died on Sara's lips. For a minute she'd forgotten that she'd only met Mike tonight. She'd done to him exactly as she'd done to Jeff many times when they'd eaten pizza at her house. But it had been with Mike, not Jeff, and Jeff's expression seemed to be reminding her of that.

"Aw, leave the widdel girl alone," Mike teased.

That broke the difficult moment. Jeff smiled and shook his head. "You have to keep these underclassmen in their place," he wisecracked. "Give 'em an inch . . ."

"I keep forgetting you're a sophomore," Peg said to Sara, as if that were a compliment.

"Yeah, I keep thinking she's a freshman," Mike said, eyeing Sara with a cocky look.

Sara growled in mock anger. "Yeah, it takes one to know one, you *fresh man*."

Mike clapped his hand over his chest. "O-w-w-w! A blow to the heart."

"You have one?" Sara asked brightly.

"Where? Where?" Peg asked, laying her hand over various spots on his chest.

"Of course he doesn't, Peg. That was just a figure of speech," Sara told Peg as if she were a teacher talking to a student.

"O-w-w-w! Another blow!" Mike cried, this time clamping his hands over the right side of his chest.

Peg and Sara laughed and crooned in fake sympathy.

"Looks like you've found someone with a sense of humor to match yours," Peg commented between giggles.

"Oh, no!" Mike exclaimed in horror. "The world couldn't take it."

Jeff seemed to be getting more sober by the minute. When the other three engaged in a duel of the forks for the last piece of pizza, he refrained. Sara, becoming aware of Jeff's strange mood, bowed out of the contest, leaving Mike and Peg to divide the piece between them.

She sipped her Coke reflectively and watched the procession of kids moving back and forth from the door to the booths or tables. Peg and Mike got into a discussion about something related to the junior class, and Sara tuned them out. She could almost feel the vibes from Jeff, sitting beside her. What was the matter with him? Was he bored? Tired? Maybe angry with her for some reason?

Someone started to move past their booth, then paused. Sara's gaze sharpened on Leslie. Leslie glanced at Jeff, frowned, and gave him a look as if he were doing something wrong. With a brief nod at Sara's table, Leslie and her date passed on toward the back of the restaurant.

Peg and Mike watched her go with expressions that looked to Sara a little less than friendly.

"Man, you were smart to call it quits on her," Mike told Jeff under his breath, then resumed his discussion with Peg.

Jeff seemed to tense up even worse and his face looked like stone. He stood up abruptly and reached for Sara's arm as he did so. She was practically forced to slide out of the booth with him.

"It's time for us to go, Sara," he said in a firm voice.

Mike and Peg looked startled. Sara glanced quickly at her watch. It was early yet! Even her dad didn't expect her home at ten. But Jeff looked so adamant, all she could do was stammer a good-night to the other two and follow after Jeff. His strides were so long she couldn't keep up. It was humiliating!

Without a word, Jeff led the way to his truck. He unlocked the passenger side and waited for Sara to get in before slamming the door. It made Sara jump. What was the matter with him? Had seeing Leslie made him act this way? Had he realized what a dud Sara—a mere sophomore—was compared to beautiful Leslie?

Jeff started the truck and headed toward home. The

drive seemed centuries long. The pickup's heater took a long time to do its job, and Sara was chilled to the bone. She tucked her face down into the turned-up collar of her coat and thrust her balled fists deep into the pockets. It didn't help much. She clamped her mouth shut to keep her teeth from chattering until the heater finally started working.

Jeff drove across the bridge to the island a little too fast, and had to brake hard as he came to the turnoff. Sara flung her arms out to keep from being dumped on the floor. That seemed to snap him out of it.

"Sorry about that," he apologized. Sara thought he sounded strained. Had she been such a dull date that Jeff was in a big rush to get her home?

"That's okay," she said in a small voice.

Soon they were at her house. The porch light was on, illuminating the walk up to the front door. Jeff escorted Sara up the four steps to the porch and stood with his back to the house, facing out toward his truck. It was like he couldn't wait to get going. Sara abandoned any idea of asking him in.

"Well, good night, Jeff," she said, managing to keep the misery out of her voice.

"Yeah." Jeff looked at her briefly and added, "Good night," almost as an afterthought. His whole body seemed poised for escape. Sara didn't want him to go; she didn't want their first date to end like this.

She heard herself say, "Thanks for asking me out, Jeff. I . . . uh . . . I really had a great time."

"Yeah, I noticed . . . especially at the pizza place," Jeff muttered. Sara frowned. It sounded like he was mad at her.

"I had a good time there," she agreed slowly. "I thought Mike and Peg were great." Maybe if she complimented him on his friends he'd get in a better mood.

That didn't happen.

"Yeah, especially Mike, huh?" Jeff spoke the words as if he couldn't help himself.

Sara was shocked. Could he be jealous of the way she'd gotten along so well with Mike? She tried to recall all that had happened that evening. It was true that she and Mike had laughed a lot together. And Sara had had a lot to say to Mike, while she'd been tongue-tied with Jeff almost all night. But Jeff jealous? That was ridiculous! He didn't have a claim on Sara, so why on earth would he be jealous? There had to be some other explanation.

"Yeah, well, maybe we can go out with them again sometime," she suggested hopefully, praying she wasn't being too bold. But she wanted to know if Jeff would ask her out again, and the words were out before she could stop them.

Jeff looked uncomfortable. First he stared out at his truck, then down at the porch floorboards, his face in the shadows. He shifted his weight on his feet. Thrusting his hands into the pockets of his jacket, he spoke with seeming reluctance. "You'd like that, huh? To go out with *Mike?*" There was heavy emphasis on Mike's name.

Sara actually began to hope Jeff was jealous after all. "No, with Mike and *Peg,*" she insisted, looking up into his face earnestly. It was hard to read his expression, since it wasn't in the light, but it appeared to Sara that the stiff planes of his cheeks and mouth softened slightly.

"Oh," he mumbled. Did he sound relieved a little? "Well, maybe we will." The end of the sentence had a tiny uplift to it, like the idea was being left up in the air. It wasn't exactly a promise of another date, but it wasn't a no, either. It was entirely unsatisfying to Sara.

There was an uncomfortable pause. Sara sought for something to say to make Jeff change the idea of a second date from a maybe to a yes, but her mind was too slow.

Jeff said softly, "Good night, Sara," and turned to

walk to his truck. Sara watched him go, her heart close to breaking.

Stay, Jeff, she wanted to call. Ask me out again. Please. Don't be mad at me. But of course she didn't say any of that. Instead she stood stock-still and watched him get into his pickup without even a glance back at her. She watched him drive away until the red taillights disappeared around a bend in the road, and then turned toward her front door. She knew on the other side of it her parents and Gram were probably waiting up to hear all about her date, but right then all Sara wanted to do was run upstairs to her room and cry. Her first—and only?—date with Jeff seemed to have ended so miserably. What had she said or done wrong? Would she ever find out?

# 4

Taking a deep breath, she grasped the cold porcelain knob and turned it. As she'd expected, the lights were on in the living room. The television was on, but its volume was low. Gram, wrapped in one of her own quilts, was slumped in the reclining chair, fast asleep. Sara's father was watching the screen but her mother was reading a book. As Sara reluctantly entered the room, she plastered a smile on her face that threatened to dissolve at any moment.

"Hi." She made her way over to Gram's footstool and sank down on it. The way she felt right then, if she didn't sit down, she'd fall down. She perched next to Gram's tiny feet, which were propped up on the stool; the toes of her quilted slippers peeked out from under the blanket.

Sara's dad turned off the TV and turned toward her

with a smile. The action proved Sara's suspicions that everyone had stayed up just to see her.

"Well, how was the movie?" her mom asked.

"Oh, it was great. James Bond saved the world again," she returned with as much nonchalance as she could muster.

"Ah, good." Her father smiled. "I can sleep well tonight."

Sara grinned on the outside, but was having trouble on the inside. Beside her, Gram stirred but didn't wake.

"Looks like you'll have to carry her upstairs," Ruth told Tom.

He smiled. "That'll be easy. She's light as a feather."

Then both parents looked at their daughter expectantly. She knew they were curious about her date. Better to get it over with and have a good chance of getting upstairs before the tears start, she thought. As quickly as possible she told them about the popcorn wars, about going to the Pizza Inn afterward, and how much she liked Jeff's friends Mike and Peg.

"So you had a nice time," her mom commented with satisfaction.

"Yes." Sara realized she didn't have to lie about that. She had had a good time on the date—until Jeff brought her home.

Tom flexed his shoulders and reached to turn out one of the lights. With relief Sara took that as a signal that she was free to go. After placing a kiss on each parent's cheek, she ran upstairs and closed her door.

She sagged against it, and all of a sudden she lost the control she'd had over her emotions. Tears burst forth like a broken dam. Tearing off her clothes, she dropped into bed and pulled the blankets over her head in an attempt to muffle the sound of her sobs. She couldn't even have the luxury of a good cry in her room for fear of waking Joy.

A small sleepy voice told her it had happened anyway.

"Sara? What's the matter?" Joy mumbled, raising her head off the pillow.

"Nothing." Sara tried to sound normal, but a tiny quiver remained in her voice that tipped Joy off.

"Then why are you crying?"

Sara gulped and tried to pull herself together.

"Huh, Sara?"

"Because Jeff didn't kiss me," Sara blurted out, and then buried her fiery hot face under the pillow. She hadn't meant to say that out loud!

There was silence from the other bed for a bit. Joy's voice registered confusion as she answered, "Oh." That was followed by a yawn, and the little girl's head dropped back down. Soon she was asleep again.

Sara suppressed a loud sob, swallowed, and stuck her head back out from under the stifling pillow. She took deep breaths and managed to get herself calmed down enough to stop crying.

The turmoil she felt inside confused her. She'd never felt this way before. Her date with Jeff had been more important to her than she would ever have expected. And its failure was more devastating than she seemed able to deal with. What had happened? Why had he suddenly acted so distant and even angry? Would he ask her out again, or had she spoiled that somehow? One last sob made her breath catch in her chest, and then she gave up trying to figure it all out, finally falling asleep.

She tried not to mope around the house over the weekend, for fear her parents would realize everything wasn't as great as she'd led them to believe. She didn't want Susy to know what a bummer the date had been either, so when Susy called to get the details, she made a big deal over the movie and pizza afterward and deliberately was hazy over the drive home. It almost worked until

Susy, who never was satisfied unless she knew absolutely everything, asked, "And did he kiss you good night?"

Sara stalled. "Susy, this was only our first date!"

"So what? You've known each other for ages, so that shouldn't make a difference. You mean he didn't kiss you?" She sounded incredulous.

"No," Sara mumbled. There were times when she wished Susy wasn't so intensely interested in everything she did, and this was one of them.

Just to get off the phone, she said, "I think Mom wants me. I gotta go. I'll see you Monday," and hung up before Susy could say anything. It wasn't really a lie, she told herself. Her mother could always use some help, and when she went downstairs to ask, sure enough, her mom put her in charge of doing some laundry.

Monday morning, as she and Susy approached the bus stop, Sara was hoping Jeff would give her some sign that everything was okay between them, but she was scared he'd treat her like she was invisible.

He didn't do either. All the others were waiting already, their backs to the wind that was blowing relentlessly across the island. A storm was brewing out in the Atlantic that would soon move up the coast. When anyone spoke, the wind tore the words away, so all Jeff did was smile—a nice wide one, Sara saw with relief—and wave. His lips moved and she knew by the shape of his mouth that he said, "Hi, Sara," but it was hard to hear clearly. She returned the greeting, smiled at Jackie, who stood at the end of the row of three boys, and took a spot next to her, with Susy bringing up the rear.

Jackie was dressed in her usual tight designer jeans and bubble jacket, and today had on a knit hat and a turtleneck with the collar pulled up over her mouth. She dragged it down to shout at Sara, "I thought I was moving *south*. Where'd the warm weather go?"

Sara laughed. "At least we don't have snow like New York does right now."

"True. But I like snow. If I'm going to have a cold March, I want the snow to go with it, so I can go skiing."

"Oh," Sara mumbled. She could hear Susy make some caustic comment next to her, and was glad no one else could tell what she said. Susy's mouth was going to get her in trouble someday if she didn't watch it.

She was glad when the bus came along. The three boys made sure Jackie was the first on, and then Stan and Pete crowded after her. Only Jeff stayed back so Sara and Susy could board.

"Creeps!" Susy muttered as she followed the two guys on.

As Sara dropped in her seat, she tried not to look up as Jeff got on. Susy slid in beside her, Jeff headed toward the back, and Sara let out a sigh. So much for hoping he'd say anything. With Susy there it would have been impossible. Sometimes she felt like she could just haul off and hit Susy.

What Sara wanted to happen finally did on Tuesday. To her total shock, when she came out of her last class for the day, Jeff was standing there waiting.

"Hi," he said, falling in step as she headed for her locker.

"Hi." She succeeded in keeping her surprise hidden.

"How's science these days?" he asked.

Sara twirled the locker combination, wondering why he'd stepped out of character like this. She was having trouble remembering the combination she'd known for over six months. "Don't ask. In lab today we were dissecting frogs."

"Great, huh?" Jeff grinned.

"Yeah, right." Sara giggled. "You know what made me the sickest? The gallbladder. Ugh, that color!"

Jeff smiled. "Yeah," he said deadpan, "and just my luck, when I took bio, my frog had gallstones."

Sara squinted at him. "But frogs . . ." Then she saw his lips quiver and realized he was teasing. She playfully hit him in the shoulder. It was hard as a rock from all Jeff's fishing work. "You have a lot of *gall* making a joke like that!" She laughed and turned toward the bus. Her heart sang. Everything was okay again! Jeff still liked her.

He followed her onto the bus and took Susy's spot next to her. Susy was usually late and Sara always saved her seat for her. Today when Jeff took it, Sara felt a little pang of guilt, but not enough to make him move! Susy rushed on at the last minute, spotted Jeff next to Sara, and flung herself into a vacant seat just as the bus started rolling. Oh, well, Sara thought, I hope she understands.

They pulled out of the school grounds and Sara glanced at Jeff. Why had he sat with her today? And then she had her answer as he asked, "You want to go see the Mariners cream Topsail Friday night?"

This was it! He'd done it. A second date!

"Yes," Sara got out happily, and then thought: What if she still couldn't think of anything to talk about around Jeff? What if she blew it a second time? Would there be a third? Maybe if there were other people with them to help fill the spaces in the conversation like last time . . .

"Will Mike and Peg be with us?" she blurted out before she realized how stupid that was.

Jeff frowned and answered stiffly, "No, but if you want, I'll ask them."

Did her mentioning Mike make Jeff mad? "No," she said quickly. "Don't do that. I was just curious."

Jeff shuffled through some papers in his looseleaf notebook. Sara thought she saw his jaw tighten, but she was pretending to be interested in what was happening on the other side of the bus.

Some guys were fooling around. They'd stolen a hat belonging to a boy who was kind of an egghead, nicknamed Brain, and were throwing it toward the back of the bus, row by row. The boy was trying to act like it was all a joke rather than viciousness. But Sara didn't like what was happening. She looked at Jeff. He still hadn't said anything and didn't seem to notice what was going on in the bus.

"Jeff?"

"Huh?" He acted like he'd just woken up.

Sara told him about the stolen hat, and as she expected, he calmly got up and went to collect the hat, returning it to its owner. She was proud of him; sometimes he seemed so much more mature than the other guys his age.

When he came back and dropped into his seat, she thanked him. He smiled and slumped against the backrest, but still didn't have anything to say. His face looked slightly troubled but Sara couldn't figure out what was bothering him. One thing did seem obvious: she was responsible for the silence between them, and if she didn't want it to last all the way home, she'd better do something about it. So what could she say that would get Jeff talking again? There was a teen magazine at home that had an article on how to talk to boys, and it had said to get them going on their interests. That's what she'd do.

"How's it going on the *Scuttlebutt?*"

Mentioning the school paper seemed to perk Jeff up. He turned toward Sara with a grin. "Great," he said. "That's why we're going to the game Friday. I have to cover it for the paper."

"Oh." Sara's heart grew heavy. Talk about put-downs. Was he saying the only reason they were going out was that covering the game was part of his job? Or was his job the reason they were going to the game instead of

something else? But then, if covering the game for the
paper was his job, why would he ask a girl along? Boys!
They were impossible for Sara to figure out. She needed
someone older and more experienced to help her. But
not her mom or Gram; they were too old to remember
what it was like to deal with guys. Besides, boys today
were probably a whole different breed compared to guys
in their day.

Someone got the "Brain's" hat again and Sara stood
up, deciding to take her frustration with boys out on
some of them. She squeezed past Jeff, who looked startled, caught the cap in midair, used it to hit the nearest
male, and then stalked back to her seat. She kept the
hat until its owner got off the bus and then tossed it
to him out the window.

It was unusual for her to do something about a situation that made her angry, instead of sitting by and letting
Jeff take care of it. Some of the guys started riding Sara
about it and Jeff had to yell, "Knock it off!" when it
got to be too much. Did he think she'd been silly? Did
he disapprove?

Their bus stop came up and as soon as they got off,
Jeff said, " 'Bye, Sara. See you tomorrow," and loped
off.

Susy came off the bus and stood beside Sara. Sara
linked her arm through her friend's and danced a little
jig. "He did it, Susy! He asked me out again."

"Oh?"

They started walking, Sara bubbling over with the details. She told Susy how relieved she was that Jeff had
asked her to the game, because guys had asked her out
before, but not always for a second date. She didn't
mention that she was also relieved because she'd been
afraid she'd made Jeff angry at her and that he'd *never*
ask her out again.

"Well, that's . . . great." Susy smiled and withdrew

her arm from Sara's to readjust the pile of books in her arms. "I've got tons of homework tonight," she said, rolling her eyes up. "I've got this huge long essay to write for English, and I hate writing."

The girls parted as Susy's turnoff came up. Susy waved and plodded down the lane toward her house. Sara watched her go, feeling depressed. Susy hadn't been exactly overjoyed with Sara's good fortune. Sara decided maybe she was still upset about having to sit in a different seat. Poor Susy. But they'd both known the day would come when they'd have boyfriends who'd want to sit with them on the bus. So Sara had been the first to get a boy who wanted to sit with her. Was that her fault? With a little shrug, Sara turned toward home. And anyway, just because Jeff chose to sit with her today didn't mean he'd do it again. Though Sara sure hoped he would.

He didn't the next day, to Susy's obvious pleasure. Jeff rode with his friends in the back of the bus, leaving Sara depressed.

In English class that day the teacher called for everyone to present the assignments. The boy who sat in front of Sara happened to be the one she'd smacked with Brain's hat on the bus. He didn't have his homework done.

"Gee, Miss Cain, my little brother needed shredded paper for his hamster cage and he took my homework."

The class broke up, but Miss Cain only smiled tightly and said, "Nice try, Tim. You get a ten out of ten for originality, but a zero for honesty. And a zero is going in my gradebook." She looked over Tim's shoulder. "Sara, do you have yours?"

"Yes." Sara rose to walk to Miss Cain's desk.

Tim turned in his seat and said snidely, "Yeah, Miss Do-Gooder always does what's right." He casually stretched one leg out in the aisle, and if Sara hadn't been looking down she'd have tripped over it. After she presented the paper to the teacher, she returned to her seat. Tim's expression as he watched her made Sara uptight. It was clear he didn't like her interference in their fun the day before. She knew she'd acted out of character. Girls seldom put the skids on whatever guys did, and Sara never had. She reflected on that. Was it her relationship with Jeff that now made her act like she never had before?

Sara related Tim's hamster-cage excuse to Susy while they waited for their bus the next morning. Jackie, who stood nearby, overheard it and said, "Man, that's another way things are so different down here. Back home we use excuses like 'The computer was down,' or 'My little brother thought the floppy disk was a record and put it on his toy stereo.' "

The boys laughed and asked her if she had a computer, while Sara sank into a gloomy mood. *Back home*, Jackie had said. It was pretty clear she didn't think of Carteret Island as home, and it was too bad, because Sara couldn't imagine a lovelier place to live. What could Long Island possibly have to make it a better place?

When Friday night finally came, Jeff collected her in his blue truck. He was dressed exactly as he had been the last time. Sara had on casual clothes too. She was learning fast.

It wasn't nearly as cold tonight. She wondered aloud, "Do you think spring will come soon?"

Jeff smiled at her, making her heart lurch. "You love spring, don't you?"

"Yeah," she said, returning his smile shyly.

"Remember that time when we were five or six and you found the first flowers of spring and got me to help you pick them for your mom?" he asked, his eyes twinkling.

Sara giggled. "Yeah, and they were old Mrs. Trimball's crocuses and Mom had to buy her new bulbs and plant them in place of the ones you pulled out by the roots!" She was pleased that Jeff shared the same memories as she.

They laughed together, then drove in silence to the school.

Sara hadn't gone to many of the Mariners' games. Basketball didn't feature in her list of favorite activities, but she wasn't going to tell Jeff that. The smell of the gym, the heat of the room, the constant buzz of noise from the crowd filled her senses as they entered. Jeff chose a seat directly behind the players' bench, but as yet none of the team was present. Amid the general hubbub, Sara sat quietly and watched Jeff kid around with some of the other guys.

Then the Carteret High Mariners, in their gold-and-blue uniforms, trotted out onto the court. Topsail came out of their side and both sides stood up and cheered their teams.

Jeff pulled a notepad from his hip pocket, and almost as soon as play began, he was scribbling away.

The first half of the game, the teams were neck and neck for scores, and at half-time they were tied. When play resumed, both high schools were going wild. The cheerleaders for each team tried to outyell, outjump, and outperform the other, urging their side to victory.

Things started looking bad when the Mariners' best scorer had one too many personal fouls called on him and had to leave the game.

"What's the matter with him tonight?" Jeff muttered disgustedly.

Topsail's best player dribbled down the court and rebounded the ball off the backboard to a teammate who arched it into the basket. Topsail kids went crazy while the Carteret kids sank into a collective depression. Sara realized with their best scorer out of the picture the rest of the team was going to have to try very hard to catch up. Now they had to make two points just to tie Topsail. She found herself gripping her seat.

Carteret got the ball and passed it among themselves. One of the players received the ball, dribbled along the extreme edge of the court to try to get near the basket and get a shot at it from the side. His back was to the court as he tried to keep the ball out of the reach of his opponent. The player guarding him crowded him so much he started to trip out of bounds at the corner. Arching his back, he threw the ball cleanly over his head to keep it in play. Just as he fell out of bounds, the ball was received by a teammate who instantly scored, sinking the ball to the screams and cheers of Carteret High.

"What a save!" Jeff yelled.

Topsail got the ball and moved down the court to their end. As he watched them passing the ball back and forth, looking for a good shot, Jeff leaned toward Sara. "There are only fifty-six seconds of play left," he announced ominously.

Sara glanced at the clock. It was true. Carteret's last basket had only tied the score again. If Topsail scored now they'd win!

The lead player for Topsail found himself with a clear shot at the basket. He raised the ball and aimed. The nearest Mariner leapt into the air and managed to deflect the ball as it left his opponent's hands. It bounced once and in a lightning move another Mariner stole the ball, dribbled furiously down the court to the home basket, and slam-dunked it. The buzzer sounded almost immediately, signaling the end of the game. The Carteret High bleachers rose to their feet, going wild.

"We won!" Sara yelled, jumping up and down.

Jeff bounced beside her, cheering. Then he turned to Sara, swept her into his arms, and twirled her around.

Before she realized what had happened, he set her back on her feet and turned to the Mariners who were congregated in front of them. He pounded the back of one of the players and pumped the hand of another. Sara stood in shock, swamped by her emotions. She felt deliriously happy, but not because the home team had won. Jeff's touch had set off little demolitions of feelings inside her that made her want to burst. Had he been carried away by the excitement of the game? Or was it something more?

There was no time to think about it. Jeff turned back to Sara and said, "I want to go to the locker room and interview a couple of the guys. I'll be back in a little while." And he was gone, bounding down the risers to follow the team into no-girl's-land.

Sara felt deflated. Was this the end of their date? When he came back, would they go home?

Desolately she sat on the bleachers while kids around her started the mass exodus from the gym. She spotted Mike's dark head next to Peg's curly blond one. They were walking arm in arm, and as they neared the door they saw her and waved. They couldn't stop to talk, though, since once you were in the herd of kids you got sucked out of the gym with the flow.

Several minutes went by. Sara fidgeted. Where was Jeff? Why did it take so long to interview a couple of guys? She began to get impatient, then angry. If he didn't come back soon, she'd leave without him and hitch a ride home with someone she knew, she told herself. But that was an empty threat. No sooner did she spy Jeff loping across the gym toward her than she melted. All her anger evaporated when he smiled at her as if he was really pleased to see her.

He held out his hand and drew Sara along with him out the gym door. "Come on or we won't get a table," he said.

"A table? Where?" Sara looked at him, startled.

"At McDonald's," he said, seeming surprised that she didn't already know. "A bunch of us usually go there after a game."

"Oh." Sara's heart did a back flip of joy. The date wasn't over!

# 5

At McDonald's they managed to find a booth. While they ate Big Macs and drank Cokes, Jeff rattled on and on about the high points of the game. It was obvious to Sara he'd really been wrapped up in it.

She remembered all the notes he'd taken, and said, "I guess you really like being on the paper, huh? I mean, you took so many notes. Just like a professional."

She leaned across the table, since there was so much noise in the place and it was hard to hear. But she heard him answer clearly.

"Yeah. As a matter of fact I've thought about becoming a sportswriter or a reporter." He delivered that matter-of-factly, not seeming to notice the effect it had on Sara.

She stopped chewing, looking at him uncertainly. Jeff saluted a friend who passed by and they exchanged the usual banter while Sara sat there thinking. That was the first time she'd ever heard Jeff talk about being anything but a fisherman after he'd graduated from high school. It had always been understood that that was what he'd do. It was what most of the guys on the island whose fathers were fishermen did. In all the years she'd known Jeff, her visions of his future had pictured him at the wheel of his own boat, turning into one of the best fishermen the island ever saw. For her part, she'd always assumed sooner or later one of the guys would notice her and they'd eventually get married and she'd stay on the island too. It had never occurred to her that Jeff didn't share the same ideas about his life after school was over.

Jeff was sipping his Coke. The friend was gone now and Sara took the moment to ask, "You mean a part-time reporter when the fishing is bad?"

Jeff's expression troubled her. He looked funny, like a kid caught stealing from the cookie jar or something. Then he acted a little annoyed. "No. I mean *instead* of fishing." He took a loud pull on his Coke, as if he wanted to drown out whatever Sara said in response.

A panicky feeling welled up inside Sara. This didn't sound at all like what she'd always expected. She didn't like the way he talked, either—almost defiantly.

"But I thought . . . I mean . . ." She groped for words, trying to express her fears.

Jeff frowned down at his hamburger, which he'd just mashed by gripping it too firmly. Catsup oozed out all over his fingers like an angry red stain. He shifted uncomfortably in his seat, and his next words came out with a hard, resentful edge.

"Not everyone is cut out to be a fisherman." Then he muttered under his breath, so softly Sara almost didn't catch it, "Or *wants* to be."

Before she could think of what to say, one of the Mariners and his girlfriend stopped by their booth to talk to Jeff. He looked so relieved, Sara knew he wanted their conversation to end.

"Hey, my man, take a seat," he invited, and the two sat down next to Jeff and Sara, who moved over to make room for them.

The four of them started the usual talk about school, and time went by quickly. Before Sara realized it, Jeff was looking at his watch and saying, "Got to get the show on the road, Sara."

They said good-bye to the others and went out to the truck.

As they began another long, silent drive home, Sara thought: Here we go again. This was the pits! Why did she have to get a terminal case of lockjaw the minute she got in this truck with Jeff? It was as if they didn't speak the same language. She had to be the dullest date he'd ever taken out. What did Jeff think?

Suddenly she found out what Jeff thought.

"I have to say this, Sara, I really like a girl who doesn't drive you nuts by talking all the time." He grinned at her. She turned beet red, not sure if he was being funny or insulting, and couldn't look at him. Then he added, "You know, some girls seem to think they have to keep up a constant stream of chatter. It can get on a guy's nerves. You're different." He smiled at her, and she realized he meant every word—as a compliment.

With a self-conscious laugh, Sara said, "Well, you couldn't have said that about me in the past. Whenever your family comes over, I always seem to have plenty of stuff to say." She turned an even brighter shade of red. How awful! How revealing! Would Jeff guess that the reason she was tongue-tied now was that she was beginning to like him as a boyfriend instead of a "buddy"? Averting her face, she pretended interest in the view out her window. She hoped the lights from the dashboard weren't bright enough for Jeff to see her burning face!

She had to say something quick to make him think otherwise.

"Well, I guess the reason I haven't been so talkative as usual is that this isn't the same thing as a dinner with our families." Oh, good grief! She'd said exactly the opposite of what she'd intended.

Jeff was slow to answer, but when he did, it was a soft, thoughtful, "Yeah."

She thought she'd die for sure now. Why couldn't she be like the Incredible Shrinking Woman and just disappear under the floor mat? How was she going to survive the drive home?

Somehow she made it. Neither spoke until they reached Sara's. She had no idea what he was thinking. But she was petrified he now knew what she was feeling and didn't want her to like him that way. Why hadn't she thought before she opened her stupid mouth?

Jeff parked in front of her house. More than anything else, Sara wanted to throw the door open and race into the house. But that would be all the proof he'd need that her words had carried a deeper meaning.

She forced herself to sit there as Jeff came around the front of the truck and opened her door. Then he did something that made her flip. Instead of standing back so she could get out, like he'd always done before, Jeff stepped forward and offered her his hand.

She stared at it, her heart in her throat. She could feel a wave of dizziness wash over her and her palms were suddenly so damp she could hardly believe it. What was the matter with her? She was practically a basket case! One thing was for sure: if Jeff felt her palm, he'd know something was wrong, too. In a flash a solution hit her. Trying to make it look like an accident, she reached for her purse, knocking it on the floor.

"Oops!" She bent down to retrieve the purse and managed to wipe one hand on her jeans. She turned back to Jeff and placed the dry hand in his. How warm and strong his felt! Strange tingles seemed to be making their way up her arm from his touch. Did Jeff feel it too?

He pulled her out of the truck. When she stood down on the ground, they were within inches of each other.

Sara looked up into his face uncertainly. Jeff looked back at her, still holding her hand. Their eyes locked, then shifted away, then locked again. Jeff looked like he wasn't exactly sure what he should do next. Sara certainly didn't know what she was supposed to do. She realized she'd been holding her breath and tried not to let it out in a whoosh. Jeff was standing between her and the house and she couldn't step around him, because the open truck door was blocking her.

Jeff seemed to realize that too. He stepped back, making room for her to head up the walk. Although she felt like a huge vise was squeezing all the breath out of her lungs with each step she took, she managed to make it to the porch, with Jeff close behind. Then she turned toward him.

"I . . . I had a great time," she said in a shaking voice. She had to get a hold of herself! "The game was fun," she added in a stronger tone. That was a stupid remark! She would have said the same thing even if Jeff had taken her to a dogfight. Anyplace Jeff took her would be great.

"I enjoyed it too, Sara. Really."

He continued to stare down at her as if she were some new kind of space being he'd just discovered on the porch.

Silence.

Now we're both tongue-tied, Sara thought.

The wind rustled the naked branches of the old walnut

tree and some of them scratched at the corner of the porch roof. The noise seemed so loud, Sara nearly jumped out of her skin. Each second seemed as long as an hour. She saw Jeff's Adam's apple move up and down as he swallowed, and then lightly his hands touched her shoulders.

"I'd like for us to go out again." It sounded like he was just learning how to use his vocal cords.

"I'd like that too." Sara's voice sounded odd too.

Then, just as surely as if they did it all the time, Jeff lowered his head and touched his lips to hers. His mouth was firm, yet soft. Warm, but not hot. The pressure was just right—kind of gentle. But firm enough to make crazy sensations run up and down Sara's back and make her knees wobbly.

Then he lifted his head. "Thanks, Sara. I'll see you." He was gone—in his truck and driving away before she woke up from her trance.

Sara was trembling. It was all she could do to get the door open and get inside the house. The thought of talking to her parents was more than she could bear.

"Sara? Is that you?" her mother's bright voice called from the living room.

Who else did she expect to come into the house at eleven o'clock at night? Sara mumbled something and rushed upstairs. She darted into the bathroom, shutting the door and locking it. She felt shaky all over. Could anyone tell she'd been kissed?

A look at herself in the mirror told the truth. Her cheeks were flushed and her eyes were so bright! Was she really going to cry?

A knock on the door made her jump. "Sara?" her mother called through the panels of the door. "What are you doing in there?"

What did she think she was doing in there? Sara thought resentfully. How many things could a person do in a bathroom? She wrenched on the tap water.

"I'm brushing my teeth. I got something stuck in them and it was driving me crazy all the way home," she called. And if you believe that one, I'll tell you another, she thought.

"Oh." Her mother sounded convinced, and said, "Well, come down when you're through."

No! Sara turned off the water and laid her head against the door. "Uh, Mom?"

"Yes?"

"Uh, could we talk about it tomorrow? I'm kind of tired. I yelled myself hoarse at the game and . . . uh . . . I don't know. Maybe I'm coming down with something." She let her voice trail off, trying to sound weak and weary—which was easy!

"Well, all right, dear." Her mother didn't sound too enthused about that, but at least she agreed. "You better get right to bed, then."

"Yeah, I will. Good night." Please go away, she added silently.

"Good night."

Sara pressed her ear against the door and heaved a sigh of relief when she heard her mother's slow, deliberate steps descending the stairs.

She waited a little longer, washed her face and brushed her teeth for real, then tiptoed to her room. She undressed in the dark and lay down on her bed, careful to avoid the spot where the springs squeaked. She didn't want Joy to wake up and spoil her evening with a lot of babyish questions.

Now she was calm again. She didn't feel like crying anymore.

Her first kiss! From Jeff, that is. But his kiss was so good, it made all those other little good-night pecks seem as exciting as a kiss from Shep, the family dog. In her imagination, she relived it a couple of hundred times. But what had it meant to Jeff? Anything? Had he thought she expected it? Would he kiss her because he thought she expected it after their second date? Or because *he* wanted to do it? Oh, this was frustrating! It seemed she was constantly trying to figure out Jeff's motivation for doing things.

She sighed and rolled over. Well, anyway, tomorrow she'd have something great to tell Susy.

Then she remembered how Jeff had talked at McDonald's. A reporter *instead* of fishing. There couldn't be much need for a reporter here on the island. So that would mean he'd have to move away. Sara had a wrenching feeling inside when she thought about that. No Jeff around in the years to come? Please don't do it, Jeff, she prayed. I want you here . . . with me . . . because I think I really care about you. . . .

She drifted off into an unrestful sleep.

Susy came over the next morning, supposedly to work on a dress she was making with Sara's help. But as soon as the girls got the portable sewing machine set up in Sara's room, Susy began pumping Sara.

"Well, how did it go? Did you have a good time? And did he kiss you?"

Sara lay back down on her bed, spread her arms, and stared at the ceiling. She sighed. "Fine. Yes. And yes! He did kiss me—"

"How many times?"

"Once."

"Once?"

"But it was really fantastic!" Sara sat up, stars in her eyes. "I mean, it was like all the other kisses I've ever had were nothing. You know what I mean?"

"Yeah." But Susy didn't sound like she *really* understood.

Maybe none of Susy's kisses have been anything because she hasn't been kissed by a boy she really cares about, Sara thought. She felt intensely sorry for Susy.

Susy turned to her sewing. "Well, that's great. Of course, I guess today almost any guy expects a kiss on the first or second date. It doesn't mean a thing to them." She started the machine and the whirring filled the silence.

She's jealous! Sara thought. But was she jealous because Sara got kissed? Or because Sara got kissed by *Jeff*?

She decided to change the subject. "So let's see the pattern instructions. I'll look up how to do those special tucks in the bodice."

Susy handed them to her, and the subject of dates, boys, and Jeff in particular was dropped.

Later that evening, Sara was sitting in the old-fashioned parlor with Gram. Gram was preparing a new skein of yarn for some knitting project, which meant Sara had to help unravel it so Gram could wind it into a ball. She didn't like the pull-skein style, insisting that a ball was better and less likely to get messed up.

Sara really loved her grandmother. She always seemed cheerful around Sara. And restful. And wise. Sara decided to tap some of that wisdom.

Trying to sound casual, she said, "Uh, Gram? Susy and I were talking today and, uh, we were thinking about how guys today seem to think you owe them a kiss just because they take you out on a date."

Gram's eyes sharpened on her. She knew Sara had been out with Jeff, but she didn't say anything except, "Oh?"

"And, well, I was wondering . . . back when you dated, how long did it take for a guy to decide to kiss you?"

Gram laughed. "As long as he wanted to wait. Which sometimes was on the *second* date." Her eyes twinkled as she looked at her granddaughter.

It was Sara's turn to say, "Oh."

She knew Gram had guessed that she'd been kissed, but was playing dumb. She decided as long as she'd gone this far, she'd go all the way. "Well, do you think it means anything? I mean, would a guy kiss a girl just for kicks, or what?"

Gram seemed to be really interested in her ball of yarn. But her voice was lively as she answered without looking at Sara, "Well, it seems to me that men have always kissed a girl for one reason. And that's because they wanted to. Now, as to the reason why they'd want to . . ." Sara held her breath. "I guess a man would have to really like the girl, because otherwise he wouldn't want to bother kissing her at all."

"Oh."

"Of course, that's just my opinion, you understand. I know kids today seem to view kissing and anything that goes with it as a right rather than a privilege." There seemed to be a hint of warning in Gram's voice and eyes as she looked at Sara, but Sara didn't care. All she could hope was that the reason Jeff had kissed her was that he really liked her. Because she didn't think he was the kind to grab a kiss just because he wanted one, not because he wanted to kiss that particular girl.

"Well, I guess the ball is done," Gram said, and Sara got up to get Joy ready for bed.

Monday morning at the bus stop, Jeff was involved in talking to the other guys. He looked up and smiled when Sara and Susy walked up, and Sara thought she saw just a hint of something special in that smile. But he didn't leave the guys this time either. She would have thought after that kiss that he'd pay more attention to her. Unless it didn't mean anything.

Sara wished desperately that Jeff would sit with her on the bus, but she didn't want to tell Susy to sit somewhere else just in case Jeff took the hint. Susy seemed to be feeling a little down lately, and making her give up her seat for Sara's love life would probably hurt her feelings and make her feel even worse.

So when the bus came, Sara and Susy sat in their usual seats. With her heart resting somewhere under her feet, Sara watched Jeff board and head down the aisle. Jackie was directly in front of him. As they passed Sara, Jackie turned to Jeff.

"Hey, man, that math had me freaking out last night. I can't get it. Sit with me and help me?" Her beautiful blue eyes gazed up into Jeff's as if he were the world's best math whiz and only he could help her, when Sara knew darn well that either of the other guys would be just as much help.

"Sure," he said, smiling. Was it Sara's imagination or did he smile just as nicely at Jackie as he had at Sara before?

Susy was chattering about something, but Sara couldn't concentrate. She pulled out her compact and pretended to be checking her makeup; then, to prolong it, she combed her hair. But she was really looking in the mirror at Jackie and Jeff. They were sitting way at the back of the bus with their heads together. They really did look terrific together. Sara felt deflated. Jeff and Jackie seemed to be talking and laughing a lot. What was so funny about math? she wondered. They probably weren't even talking about math! Sara wanted to cry. Then she brought herself up short. What was she getting so uptight about? So all right. Jeff and Jackie were friends. It made sense, didn't it? After all, they were both juniors and had a lot of classes in common. And guys could have girls who were friends without them having to be *girlfriends*, right?

Then she really felt awful. Up until two weeks ago that was all she and Jeff were—friends, plain and simple. Did two dates and one kiss really change all that? Yes!

The answer was deeply etched in her heart. For her it had. Very much. She really had to admit it—she was crazy about Jeff. Maybe this was love and maybe it wasn't, but one thing was for sure: she hadn't a clue as to how he felt about her. No matter what Gram said, she really didn't know how much Jeff cared about her. Would she ever?

Susy asked her a question. Sara had been paying her half-attention and was able to answer it and stop torturing herself with her doubts about Jeff. Until later.

During school she spotted Jackie with a girlfriend walking down the hall. They were headed toward the cafeteria, and Sara heard a snatch of the conversation.

"Lemme tell you, this guy is such a fox. I mean, back home he'd have his pick of girls," Jackie was saying.

"Wow! And all this time I kind of ignored him . . ." the other said, and then they turned into the cafeteria and Sara couldn't hear any more.

Were they talking about Jeff? If they were, Sara had to admit Jeff was a fox. And was Jackie trying to win him over? That wouldn't be hard.

Later in the day she saw Jeff and Jackie walking down the hall together. They had their heads bent toward each other as if they were saying something they didn't want anyone else to hear. Sara's heart plummeted. Darn that Jackie! Why did she have to move here just when Sara was starting to get Jeff to notice her? Jackie couldn't make Jeff as happy as Sara could. Why, they were from two different worlds! Jackie was so . . . so modern. Jeff had lived here all his life. He didn't need her coming down here and messing it up.

Sara stewed about that the rest of the day, and by the time she headed for the bus she was so low she felt as though she'd have to look up to see people's shoes. She wasn't really concentrating on where she was going and she almost ran into Jeff and Jackie. Jeff and

Jackie. Why did those two names have to sound so good together?

"Hi, Sara," Jackie said brightly. She actually looked like she was glad to see Sara. "How's it going?"

"Uh, fine," Sara mumbled, feeling terrible for the way she'd been thinking about Jackie all day. She was a rat!

Jackie turned to Jeff and Sara thought she had a secret look in her eyes for Jeff alone. It was like she was sending him a message. "See you. Thanks for that math help; it saved my hide."

She turned and boarded the bus and didn't seem to care whether Jeff followed her, which Sara thought was strange.

Sara smiled tightly at Jeff and climbed the steps to the bus. He was right behind her. Sara sank down in her customary seat, prepared to save the spot next to her for Susy, and was shocked when Jeff dropped into it. She tried not to look as surprised as she felt.

Jeff smiled at her and she found herself thinking it was kind of a shy smile, as if he wasn't sure of his welcome. That was crazy! He was welcome to sit with her anytime. She smiled back widely and he relaxed. Then she really flipped out when he reached over and picked up her hand in his.

I'm like a roller coaster, she thought. One minute I'm up; the next I'm down. And all because of Jeff. If he doesn't pay attention to me, I'm flat out in the dirt. But if he does, I'm high up in the clouds!

# 6

The bus started rolling and then had to stop as Susy came flying up to it, hammering on the door. Amid catcalls she hopped in and her face fell as she saw Jeff in her seat. Sara felt awful. Had Jeff noticed? She was afraid to look. Susy found a seat, squeezing in with a couple of girls she was fairly good friends with, and Sara felt herself relax. Well, Susy would have to get used to it if Jeff did this again. And she hoped he would.

She sneaked a look at him; he was gazing in Susy's direction. Was he thinking about her, too? Had Susy's presence been what had kept him from sitting with her before?

Then suddenly he turned to her. "Hey, want to take in a flick Friday?"

Sara was momentarily startled. Not because he'd asked her for a date. That was terrific! But she frowned as she realized what word he'd used for "movie"—"flick." There was only one person she knew who used that term. Jackie. It was obvious Jeff had been spending a lot of time around her if he was beginning to pick up her vocabulary.

But there was no time to stew about that. "Yeah. I'd like that."

"Great. They finally changed the show," he joked.

"Oh, yeah? Which one is playing?"

Jeff shrugged and grinned. "I don't know. Does it matter?"

Sara wanted to throw her arms around him and hug him. "No," she said, laughing. Any movie with him would be perfect.

"I'll pick you up at the usual time . . ." Oh! Did that sound wonderful, Sara thought. *The usual time.* Like this was routine. ". . . and maybe we can get a pizza after."

Then he let go of her hand and searched through his notebook for a minute. He drew out the latest copy of the *Scuttlebutt* and gave it to her. "Did you see my piece on the game last week?"

"No." Sara took it, aware of a gleam of pride in his eyes. She read it and was very impressed. It really did sound professional. She complimented him on it and handed the paper back.

Then he talked about an incident that had happened at lunch that day, a dispute that had involved two guys and a teacher. The usually long ride home seemed to breeze by. Being with Jeff made that happen.

When the bus drew to their stop, Jeff and Sara got off and waited for Susy. Jeff went out of his way to be nice to Susy, Sara thought. Susy beamed as they walked together, with Jeff in the middle, asking her about one thing or another. By the time they came to the spot where Susy left them, she was laughing. When Susy said good-bye to Sara she didn't seem mad that Sara hadn't saved her a seat on the bus. Maybe Susy just needed to know that she wouldn't be left completely out in the cold if I went out with Jeff, Sara thought.

Jeff walked her home, which was really out of his way, since he should have turned off the road first; then he held her hand a little bit longer than necessary as they said good-bye. He glanced at the house and then loped off. She wondered if he'd have kissed her again if it wasn't broad daylight and there wasn't a chance that someone was in the house watching. She turned and floated into the house.

Mrs. Wilson was in the kitchen. The smell of brownies told Sara what she was up to. She placed her books on the steps and went to talk to her mother.

"Hi, Mom," she said with a peck on her mother's cheek.

"Hello, sweetie. Have a good day?" Her mother always greeted Sara that way when she came home from school, and Sara liked it. She knew her mother loved it when she sat down and talked about her day, but today she didn't want to talk about school.

"Jeff sat with me on the bus and asked me to go to the movies with him Saturday night. Okay?"

Ruth looked at her closely as she set a cup of hot chocolate before her. "Three times, Sara? My, is something going on here?" She smiled and her voice held a teasing quality that caused Sara to relax.

"I don't know." She paused, then took a deep breath and burst out, "What do you think? If a guy asks you out three times, does that mean he kind of likes you?"

She watched her mother anxiously as Mrs. Wilson made herself a cup of tea and then sat down opposite Sara at the table.

"Well, I can't imagine a boy asking a girl out three times if he didn't like her," she said slowly. "But how *much* he likes her takes time to find out."

Sara sighed. That was the trouble. That was the thing she really needed to know, and it didn't seem anyone was really able to tell her except Jeff. And so far he was not exactly opening up. Then she thought of the *Scuttlebutt.*

"Uh, Mom, does Mr. Moore expect Jeff to join him in the family fishing business after he graduates?"

"Of course. That's always been the plan." Her mother looked startled by this apparent change of topic, looking at her daughter under raised eyebrows.

Sara bit her lip. "And as far as you know, that's still the plan?"

"Yes. Why do you ask?"

"Just wondered," Sara answered evasively. She could tell by her mom's expression that she'd already hinted at too much and knew she'd better get out of the room or her mother would have her spilling the beans. She wasn't ready to voice her fears, and she wasn't completely sure she wasn't making a mountain out of a molehill. After all, Jeff could change his mind. And maybe it was all a lot of talk; maybe he knew deep down inside that his dad expected him to take up fishing and he was just trying to act like he had a choice. But he didn't, did he?

Sara stood up quickly. "I have so much homework— I think all the teachers had some kind of a contest going today to see who could assign the most. I better get started on it or I'll be up all night." She fled the kitchen before her mother could object.

Once she was in her room she spread out her books and opened her notebook, but she couldn't concentrate on her work. She found herself staring out the window by her desk instead of down at her books. Her mother said Jim Moore still expected, even planned, on Jeff taking up fishing after high school. So why did it look like Jeff had other plans? And did he really mean it? Did he really think seriously that he'd go away and become a newspaper reporter? It certainly looked like it. A sharp pain began building near her heart. If Jeff wanted to be a newspaperman, he'd have to go to college first. And after college, who knew where he'd live? Not on this little island, for sure! And then she'd lose him forever—*if* she ever got him. She tried to make herself feel better by reminding herself that college for Jeff was still one and a half years away. There was plenty of time to get Jeff to like her as much as she liked him.

After supper that evening Sara got it into her head to surprise her family with a cherry-cobbler dessert. She had just pulled it from the oven when a knock came on the front door.

She heard voices as her dad greeted the caller and then her heart leapt into her throat as she identified the second voice as Jeff's. Why was he here? To see her? She wondered if she ought to stay in the kitchen or go out and act surprised that he was there. Finally, when it looked like no one was going to come get her, she made her way down the hall and looked into the living room.

Jeff was talking to her dad, who held a piece of fishing gear. "He said you can borrow it as long as you want. He's got two, so there's no rush."

"Thanks, Jeff."

Jeff glanced toward the door, spotted Sara, and said, "Hi."

"Hi."

They stood there awkwardly a second, and Sara got a brainstorm. "I was just doing the last of my science in the kitchen, and there's something I could use some help on. Do you have a minute?"

Jeff smiled widely. "Sure."

"Great. Come on back with me and I'll show you." Sara turned and retraced her steps to the kitchen with

Jeff on her heels. Once there, she dragged out the lab sheet she'd been trying to finish up from school that day, and even though there wasn't a thing on it that had given her trouble, she asked Jeff about a certain experiment. While he was explaining it to her, Ruth came into the kitchen.

"Sara, if there's plenty of that cobbler, why don't we share it with Jeff?"

Sara looked at her mom, gratitude in her heart that her mother had thought of another way to prolong Jeff's visit.

"Sure." Then she slid a look at Jeff sideways. "That is, if he's h-u-n-g-r-y," she teased.

Jeff's eyes crinkled up as he made a big deal of sniffing the aroma in the air. "Oh, I guess I could squeeze in a small piece." Both of them laughed and Sara went to the cupboard to get out the bowls. She dished out the warm dessert, topped the servings with vanilla ice cream, and helped her mother serve the adults in the living room where they were watching TV. She and Jeff stayed in the kitchen.

They ate in silence for a while, as Sara pretended to be putting the finishing touches on the lab report.

Then Jeff put his spoon down and said, "That was great. You know, you really are a good cook." He looked right at her, making her blush.

"Thanks." Her mouth felt frozen. The way Jeff was looking at her made her feel all jumpy.

She stood and took their bowls to the sink. When she came back, she dropped into her seat and looked at Jeff. She didn't need his help with her homework any-more, and soon he'd go. But in the worst way she didn't want him to go.

Jeff stared at her with a funny expression on his face, and just as Sara opened her mouth to say something—anything!—he opened his. But the sound they both heard was laughter from the front room. It reminded Sara that they weren't alone, and it frustrated her.

Jeff glanced quickly in the direction of the living room and then looked at Sara. He cleared his throat and said in a low voice, "Do you still like to take walks at night?"

"Yeah," Sara said huskily.

"Would you like to take a walk now?"

"Yes." Would she ever!

Sara got up and went to the hall closet to get her coat. Jeff was right there, helping her put it on. It made her feel like a princess. As they neared the door to the living room, she suddenly felt shy about telling her parents they were going for a walk.

As she stepped into the room, she got an idea. "Guess I'll take Shep for a walk. I feel like getting some fresh air." She looked at her parents only briefly, not wanting to see if they fell for her line. "Shep?" she called, and the dog lifted its head. When she stepped toward the door he bounded to his feet and trotted over.

She led the dog down the hall, saying over her shoulder, "Jeff's leaving now, and I guess I'll walk partway with him." Boy, talk about thinking fast! She'd probably set a record.

Jeff smiled at her as she joined him, and called, " 'Bye, Mr. and Mrs. Wilson, Gram."

Amid a chorus of good-byes they left the house, Shep leading the way. They let the dog take the lead outside, too, and didn't care when he headed across the road to the large open field.

As they came to the culvert that separated the field from the road, Jeff took Sara's hand to help her across and then didn't let go. They walked side by side for a while, hand in hand. Sara was thrilled. She felt like dancing, or throwing her arms wide and twirling around. But she'd have to let go of Jeff's hand to do that, so she resisted the happy urge.

It was a clear night, but without a moon, and it was dark. The air seemed chilly, but not too cold. It was the invigorating kind that made you feel clean inside when you took a deep breath. Sara looked up at the stars and said, "Remember when we used to lie out under the stars at night and try to count all of them? And you always claimed you'd already counted the ones I was counting and I was counting double?"

Jeff chuckled. "Yeah, and you always ended up so mad at me you pulled my coat over my head and stomped home in a fit." He laughed at that.

"Trust you to remember all my bad moments," Sara scolded.

She stopped to finger a bush. It had tight buds that she knew would be opening during the next month. "You know, I really love the island. Even in winter there's something so beautiful about it." She turned to Jeff.

"Yeah," he agreed, but added, "and small." He sounded dissatisfied about something. It made all the doubts she'd been having earlier in the day resurface.

She spoke a little too loudly as she tried to trample down her fears. "Well, at least you men can get out on your boats on the ocean. Plenty of space out there."

"Yeah." Somehow the way Jeff said that made it sound like that was a negative, not a plus. The grip he still had on her hand tightened, but Sara didn't think it was on purpose. "But not everyone becomes a fisherman." He spoke roughly, as if he were having a hard time getting the words out.

Here it comes, Sara thought in apprehension.

"I mean, look at Marshall Fuller and Jim Stokes. After they graduated they went on to college and they told me it was the best decision they ever made. And where are they now? Out there somewhere, making a *living*." His free arm made a sweep in the general direction of the mainland. His words sounded so bitter! Sara was frightened. It was as if he thought "out there" was a better place than here. Her fear escalated when he muttered, "And making a living's not such a bad idea."

He really did plan on leaving the island! It wasn't just a fantasy. All that talk about college and newspapers and being a reporter—it was for real! Suddenly Sara's fears became a cold thing lying in her heart. She began to shake all over. He'd go away and leave her! She just couldn't bear that!

"Sara? Sara?" Jeff was looking at her oddly. "What's the matter? Are you cold? Isn't that jacket warm enough?"

He sounded so concerned. Sara looked at him and mumbled, "Yeah, it's cold." Cold *inside*.

They stopped walking. Jeff wrapped his arms around her and held her close. She should have felt better, warmer, but she actually felt worse.

She started shaking again and Jeff turned them toward the house. "Come on. We'd better get back home."

But neither took that first step. Shep sat down at their feet, looking up as if he couldn't figure them out.

Jeff's arms crushed her against his chest and he kissed her. This time Sara didn't simply stand there and get kissed. She kissed him back. Hard! Maybe if she could tell him in actions what she was afraid to tell him in words, he'd realize he was just as crazy about her as she was about him. And then he'd never be able to even think of leaving the island—and her—for college and a life far away. . . .

Suddenly Jeff was pushing her away from him. Actually pushing her away! She felt hurt. "Sara, I'd better get you home." His voice sounded worried.

Sara couldn't understand why. It wasn't all that late. Her parents were used to her taking long walks; they wouldn't be concerned for a while yet.

"Come on," he said in a rough voice. He began walking, with her in tow. She didn't have any other choice but to follow him. Shep realized where they were headed and bounded off. He beat them to the door and was patiently waiting when they climbed the steps to the porch.

Sara was feeling so awful, she couldn't look at Jeff. He turned her face up to his, and ran his fingertips over her cheeks. Then he traced her chin. The look in his eyes made her melt.

"Little Sara. You're sweet," he murmured, and with a brief kiss, he left. He'd disappeared into the darkness before she even let her breath out.

Sara turned the knob and walked into the house. She didn't know what to feel. Elated? Or full of dread?

The next morning Jeff did something he'd never done before. He came to Sara's house to walk her to the bus stop.

When her mother came to tell Sara he was there, her tone of voice and the expression on her face showed Sara what she thought of this new development. Both of them knew he had to go out of his way to collect Sara. If he were willing to do that, then it must be a good sign.

Her heart pounded as Sara walked down the hall to where Jeff stood stiffly by the front door.

"Hi." She wasn't able to keep the surprise and curiosity out of her voice.

"Hi." Jeff's eyes lighted on Sara, then looked over her shoulder at her mother, who'd followed her. "I . . . uh . . . thought we could walk to the bus stop together."

"Okay." Sara took her coat from the closet, put it on, and joined Jeff. They said good-bye to her mom and headed out the door.

As they walked down the road, Sara couldn't stop herself from asking, "This is kind of out of your way, isn't it?"

Jeff shrugged. "A little." He grinned at her. "But I need the exercise."

Sara could see he was going to be evasive. "Oh? Fishing on weekends isn't enough?" she teased.

That subject didn't seem to set too well with Jeff. "No," he said with a frown. "That's just work."

Sara decided she'd better drop it. Better to simply enjoy Jeff's surprise call in case it was the last time.

But it wasn't. He showed up at her house the rest of the week, and by Friday Sara decided he intended for this to be a regular routine with them. He also sat with her on the bus, forcing Susy to fend for herself. Obviously Susy couldn't fail to notice what was happening, but for the first three days she kept quiet about it. Then on Friday at lunch she complained.

"I wish my last class wasn't on the exact opposite side of the school from the buses. At least if I was closer I'd have a better chance of getting on the bus early and getting a regular seat. I hate being the last to rush on and having to choose from the leftovers or sitting three in a seat with some girls."

Sara stabbed at the unrecognizable food item on her tray and frowned. She didn't like the peevish sound in Susy's voice. She ought to be glad for Sara.

"I wish you could sit with Jeff and me, but he's too big," she said in an attempt to smooth things over.

"Yeah." Susy glanced over at the table where Jeff still sat with the juniors.

Sara followed her line of sight, experiencing the letdown feeling she got every time she saw him over there. Why didn't he offer to sit with her? Or have her sit with him? She dragged her attention back to Susy.

"Well," she said stoutly, "soon you'll probably have a boy want to sit with you. If he takes the same bus."

"Ha!" Susy snorted. "First I have to get one to ask me out. Which *never* happens anymore. Besides, all the guys around here are losers. I don't care if they never ask me out," she claimed with an I-don't-care look on her face.

Sara wasn't fooled; she knew deep down inside Susy really did care. But she couldn't think of any pointers to give Susy to help her get dates without sounding like she was putting down her friend. Susy really needed to work on being more cheerful and less grumpy. She had a pretty face; if she'd just look happier, Sara was sure she'd attract some guy.

"Well, I guess I'm going to have to find someone *else* to save me seats from now on," Susy continued with an injured air. "Now that it's obvious you've got a permanent boyfriend."

A permanent boyfriend—that sounded so nice. But was it true? Sara wondered, gazing longingly at Jeff. He hadn't kissed her since Monday night. When they were on the bus he held her hand, but he never held it in front of the other kids. And he was still sitting way over there on the other side of the cafeteria. Didn't he want anyone to know about Sara and him? Was he a boyfriend? Or was this simply an added phase to their old boy-and-girl friendship?

# 7

The movie that Friday evening was only fair, but Sara didn't care. Jeff held her hand or put his arm around her all night—right in front of the other kids. Sara pretended she wasn't aware that others had noticed the way they were glued to each other, but it was so great to get that kind of attention, she couldn't stop herself from grinning foolishly all night. That is, when Jeff wasn't kissing her, which seemed like every twenty minutes. Whenever the action got dull on the screen, it picked up in their seats.

Afterward they went for a pizza. Sara felt like she was walking inches above the ground as they made their way over to the Pizza Inn. Once inside, they took a booth with Jeff sitting right next to Sara instead of across from her. They ordered, and then talked about all sorts of things. It was almost like old times, with a lot of silly joking, yet it was different. The air between them seemed to crackle with something. Jeff liked her—she was sure of it. The way he looked into her eyes when he talked told her that. She was in heaven just sitting there with him.

And then something happened to ruin all that.

"Hi, Jeff," a voice said. It was Bill Jarvis, a junior and a fellow reporter for the *Scuttlebutt*. Sara's spirits sank like an anchor in the ocean.

"Hi, Bill," Jeff said as Bill slid into the seat opposite them without an invitation.

"No seats left; d'ya mind?" Bill asked without seeming to expect an answer. He nodded at Sara. "Hi," he said as if greeting her took precious time he didn't like squandering.

The waitress zipped over, plopped their pizza down, and took off. Jeff and Sara looked at the pizza, then at Bill.

"I ordered over at the counter and told them to bring my stuff here. Go ahead," Bill explained.

Sara fumed inwardly. He'd been pretty sure of his welcome to do that! She took a piece and then concentrated on getting the tip of the pizza into her mouth as if it took all of her physical abilities to accomplish that.

Jeff scooped up a piece, took fully a quarter of it in one bite, and Bill took control of the conversation.

"Saw your piece in the paper about the game. Nice."

"Thanks," Jeff mumbled through his pizza, but he sounded pleased.

"Did you turn in that editorial yet?" Bill asked.

Sara thought: What editorial? She looked at Jeff.

He smiled. "Nope. I want to do a little more rewriting, and then I'll turn it in."

"Mr. Thomas said he thought your sports piece was really great. Made the game come alive for your readers."

Jeff's smile got bigger. "He did?" He hunched forward, temporarily forgetting the pizza on his plate. "What do you think he'll say about the editorial?"

"Don't know," Bill said with a grin. "But I do know it's gonna start a revolution at the least." Both guys broke up while Sara sat there feeling and probably looking dumb.

She touched Jeff's arm lightly. "What are you talking about?" She felt bad that she even had to ask. Why hadn't Jeff talked about this editorial to her?

He turned toward her. "I wrote a piece on the move by the school board last week. You know, where they voted to cut back expenditures on sports equipment and make the guys buy their own? I think they should know how the students feel about that."

Sara's eyes widened. "You mean you're allowed to write about stuff like that without getting into trouble?"

That seemed to make the guys lose control. "Oh, you're allowed to write anything you want," Jeff said between snorts. "But whether it's without getting into trouble . . ." He left that up in the air and Bill started snickering again.

"I've seen your piece. There'll be trouble all right," he said on a note of warning. But both guys were grinning.

Sara couldn't figure out what was so funny. Perhaps if she read the piece Jeff was talking about she'd understand better. But since he hadn't even told her about it, she felt reluctant to ask to see it. Maybe he hadn't mentioned it for a good reason. Or maybe she was nuts to think their relationship was so good that he felt obligated to tell her everything. Suddenly she felt unsure about things between her and Jeff again. Maybe he didn't like her better than any other girl and was just taking her out until someone else came along. Like Jackie? she wondered. But if he'd wanted to take Jackie out, why hadn't he done it yet? Or had he? Maybe on the nights he hadn't been out with Sara he'd been seeing Jackie. But if that were true, why had he kissed her? Was it because, as Susy said, some boys just felt that came with the date automatically?

Her throat hurt and her heart ached. The pizza suddenly seemed to be too gooey to control and it fell out of her fingers and onto the plate. She wiped her mouth with her napkin as if that was what she'd intended to do and listened to the guys.

They talked about the paper a little bit more while she sipped her Coke, and then Bill asked, "How are you doing looking for colleges? Did you decide yet?"

Now Sara wanted to faint. Colleges? Jeff? With a real struggle she tried not to stare at him.

"Kind of. I think it'll have to be the U. of North Carolina branch at Wilmington. I'd need to come home on weekends and help Dad. His back's really been giving him trouble lately, and he can't afford to hire anyone to help him. Not with the economy like it is."

"Yeah. My dad said the same thing. He can't replace me and he can't afford to send me to college either. Boy, I envy you," he said with spirit. "How are your folks swinging it?" He looked at Jeff curiously.

Sara was totally stupefied by now. Jeff had spoken to his parents about college? She couldn't believe it. Her family would be sure to know if that were the case.

Jeff scowled and wiped his mouth with a short angry swipe of the napkin. "That's the problem. They can't afford it either. I'm looking into scholarships now. My grades aren't great, but they're not lousy either. Mr. Carter told me he'd see if there were any special ones I might qualify for. But they'd never pick up the whole tab. I'd still need bread of my own." He looked totally defeated. Sara wanted to slip her hand into his and try to reassure him. But secretly she didn't want things to work out for him. She wanted him to stay on the island forever! Why couldn't he be happy with that, too?

Jeff and Bill moved on to other topics, while Sara stewed over the problem of Jeff going away. Soon it came time for them to go home and they rose to put on their coats.

"Let me know what happens with the scholarship thing," Bill said.

"Yeah, I will," Jeff assured him.

Sara thought: Let me know, too, so I'll know when to hang up all my dreams.

As they went back to Jeff's truck, Sara felt like she was moving in slow motion. Or maybe everything else was just moving too fast. Like Jeff's plans for the future.

Jeff didn't seem to be aware of Sara's mood on the way home, as he kept up a running commentary of stuff about school. He was talkative tonight, Sara thought. Maybe he thought if he kept talking fast she wouldn't break in and question him about college.

Unexpectedly, as if he knew there was a need to clear the air, Jeff said, "You know I really want to go to college, don't you?"

Sara nodded, not trusting herself to speak without making the way she felt deep down inside obvious to Jeff.

"Well, uh, I haven't told my folks about it yet."

Her head whipped up as she looked at him in shock. "You haven't?"

"No. I wanted to get everything squared away before I approached them about it. You know, get all the details ironed out first?" He sounded defensive. Did he expect Sara to give him a hard time about it?

"Oh," was all she could get out.

"Could you kind of keep quiet about it for now?"

"Sure." I'll definitely keep quiet about that!

"Thanks. I . . . uh . . ." He floundered around a second and then stated, "I'm sick of fishing! I mean, I'm sick of working so hard for nothing. I like the work; I really do. But there has to be a better way to pay the bills and then have some left over for little extras." He looked at her as if he were begging for her to understand.

Sara did understand that. She could see that you had to do more than just pay the bills—to simply survive. She told him so, and he smiled at her, reaching for her hand, and held it as he drove single-handedly across the bridge to the island. But instead of going all the way home right away, he found a place in the road that widened out and pulled over. He reached for her and tugged her into his arms. "You're too far away," he said with a smile in his voice, and the next several minutes were awfully quiet in the truck. But Sara loved the silence!

Then Jeff started the truck and took her the rest of the way home. Maybe things would work out, she thought hopefully after they said good night. Maybe he really was beginning to like her—*and* he could find a way to make enough money to stay on the island. She felt that if Jeff left the island, she'd lose him. But if he stayed, he'd be hers.

A week later the families had their monthly combined dinner. This time it was Jeff's family hosting. Even though Sara knew his parents must be aware he was dating her, she wondered how they'd greet her. She fretted all the way over, hoping they wouldn't say anything to embarrass her. But she needn't have worried. Stewie and Robbie were so rambunctious, no one really said anything to her at all. Doris was bustling around trying to herd the boys out from underfoot and Jim simply said, "Hi, everybody," and then the two fathers disappeared to watch some sports event on TV.

Sara wondered how the Moores could turn out a nice normal son like Jeff and two brats like Stewie and Robbie. She was glad when Joy trailed off after them, making a pest of herself. At least the Wilsons had a way of getting even, she thought gleefully, and then felt ashamed of herself for thinking of her adorable little sister as a weapon of revenge.

Jeff grabbed her hand and sneaked off with her on a long walk until dinnertime. If they were missed, no one said anything. But during dinner the conversation got a little hairy.

Tom Wilson and Mr. Moore were discussing fishing as usual, complaining about the weather this winter. A number of storms had been sweeping up the coast, playing havoc with the fish. The rough water had made it difficult to find where they'd gone.

"Things have got to improve," Jim Moore remarked.

"Yep. It's getting harder and harder to make a decent living, I'll admit," Sara's father complained.

"That's for sure. But all things considered, there's still nothing that can beat being out in the salt air, pitting your skills against nature."

They went on and on in that vein, while Jeff just sat there as if he'd turned to stone. Sara wondered when he planned to tell his folks about his desire to go to college. She could tell from the way his dad spoke that even though he considered it a hard living, he still felt fishing was tops. And he was proud of his son's abilities because from time to time he'd brag about Jeff's strength and agility on the boat. Even at those times, with everyone beaming fondly at him, Jeff's smile seemed faked.

After dinner Sara and Jeff helped Doris with the dishes, drying and putting them away, while Sara's mom helped clear the table. Jeff and Sara got talking about homework.

"Is old Lizard Neck doing her end-of-the-year push?" Jeff asked with a grin.

Sara rolled her eyes. "Is she! We have to look up all these new vocab words and copy down their definitions. Talk about grade-school work. I feel like I have to spend every weekend reading the dictionary."

Jeff turned away to place a platter he'd just dried in the cupboard. "I wish all I had to do on weekends was read the dictionary," he muttered disgustedly.

Sara's breath caught as she saw the look his mother shot him. But Mrs. Moore didn't say anything; she just washed the next dish with a lot of unnecessary concentration.

"It seems like all the teachers turned mean at the midyear, and now I'm finding the work harder," Sara remarked to cover the difficult moment.

"I know what you mean," Jeff sympathized as he took a dish from her. "Hey, why don't we do our homework together evenings and I can help you out?"

"That would be great," Sara agreed happily, thinking about all those wonderful nights ahead of them.

A loud noise from the room over the kitchen made them both glance up at the ceiling. Stew and Rob were fighting. The sound of bodies rolling on the floor and Joy shrieking told everyone downstairs that things had gotten physical. The boys' father bellowed up the stairs and there was only a partial dimming of the noise. With that kind of a racket going on, Sara couldn't imagine how they'd ever be able to concentrate. Joy was so good during her study time, Sara was spoiled.

"Listen!" she said brightly. "Why don't we study at my house. That way my parents won't worry about me walking home after dark and you wouldn't have to walk with me."

They exchanged a look that showed they both knew perfectly well Sara had suggested that to get away from the boys.

"That's a great idea," Jeff said, a lopsided smile on his face.

Neither had realized that their mothers had been listening to this exchange until Doris joked to Mrs. Wilson, "The way things are going, I guess I'll have to get used to being the mother of two, instead of three."

"Yes," Sara's mother returned. "Looks like you'll be losing a son, and I'll be gaining one. I hope he doesn't eat much."

"Oh, I doubt it. When Jim was courting me, he hardly ate a thing." Both women laughed, and Doris added, "Just send me the bill at the end of the month."

Sara blushed from the roots of her hair to her toes. She felt so flustered she almost dropped a casserole dish and Jeff had to rescue it from her. He set it aside and took her towel away, placing it with his on the drying rack.

"Well, if you're going to pick on us, I guess Sara and I'll be leaving." He took her hand and pulled her out of the kitchen despite the good-natured protests of their mothers.

They began studying together the next night. Jeff came over after dinner and stayed until nine-thirty. As he was collecting his books to go, he said, "I wanted to take you out this weekend, but Dad said I'm not spending enough time on my schoolwork since I'm fishing with him on Saturday and going out with you on Friday. He said I have to stay in this Friday and do some booking and work with him on Saturday." His face clouded and he shook his head angrily. "I wish he'd stop hounding me about fishing, fishing, fishing! That's all he talks about. You'd think the world revolved around all the fish he caught instead of other things."

"But for your dad, that's true," Sara protested.

"Huh?" Jeff looked at her puzzled.

"For him the world does revolve around fishing. It's all he's known all his life. It's how he puts meals on your table and clothes on your back and—"

She was cut off by an angry wave of Jeff's hand. "Sara! I thought at least you'd understand."

She felt cut to the heart. He sounded so condemnatory. Like she'd just admitted she was dealing in drugs at school or something.

"But, Jeff, there's nothing wrong with fishing. It's a good life and you know it."

"How many times have you heard your father spout that?"

"What?"

"Forget it," Jeff said shortly, and packed his books, turning toward the hall. He spoke with a funny voice. "You have to grow up sometime too, Sara. There's more to this world we live in than all the stuff our parents have known all their lives. It's time to look around and see what the world has to offer. When we're out of school and having to work for a living, it'll be too late to look around and try things." He sounded both bitter and wistful. Sara was perplexed by his words. He sounded so dissatisfied with the life they'd always known and shared. Why? It *was* a good life. Oh, sure, it was hard at times. Like right now when they couldn't afford a new coat for Sara to last out the rest of winter and she had to make do with the old one till spring. But there were the good times, too. Like being out on the ocean in the boat and seeing nothing but miles and miles of sky and water. And then, off to the horizon, a school of fish would suddenly appear. It was so thrilling to see

the water come alive with life. Surely Jeff still appreciated
that? Sara looked at his unhappy face, and doubts sur-
faced in her mind like one of those schools of fish. Maybe
those temporary joys weren't enough for him. But why?

Jeff left after a short kiss which made Sara almost wish
he hadn't bothered. If he was going to act like that every
time she tried to defend fishing, maybe she'd better keep
her mouth shut.

The next day at the bus stop, Sara and Jeff arrived
just in time to hear Jackie complaining to Stan Love,
"My dad came down here because he heard the fishing
was great. Well, he heard wrong! It's lousy! I wish we'd
never moved. I need new threads and the old man claims
we gotta keep what bread we have for his nest egg."
She groaned out loud and looked up at the sky. "And
even if he could afford some new clothes, there's nothing
down here like back home. It freaks me out how this
place is stuck in a time warp!"

"Ah, poor little girl," Stan crooned, attempting to put
his arms around Jackie. "Here, let me console you."

She smoothly sidestepped him and moved so Jeff was
between her and Stan. "At last, someone who understands," she said dramatically.

Jeff took the cue, raised himself up on tiptoes, and
glowered down at Stan. "Bug off, meathead," he said
good-naturedly.

"Oh, yeah? What are you? Her protector? Buzz off
yourself, dog face."

Both guys were only fooling around and a contest
began to see who could come up with the best insult.
This infantile exercise lasted until the bus came and
then continued once they were seated. That was one
thing that bothered Sara about Jeff. Whenever he was
around the guys at the bus stop, he acted as crazy as
they did. But when he and she were alone, he was a
whole different person.

On the bus Sara sat oblivious of the verbal warfare around her. She was thinking about Jackie's words. Her dad must share the same opinion of the present state of fishing as Jeff. It *was* bad, but it had been bad before. Sara could remember a time when things were so tough her family had been lucky to eat two meals a day, never mind three. But that had changed and the fishing had gotten good again. So it would change again. This temporary setback would end. She was sure of it. And when it did, would Jeff give up his college plans?

Sara decided that all she had to do was play a waiting game. Eventually everything would work out. She felt slightly better, having made a decision, and she turned her attention to the word war to see who was coming out on top. As she expected, Stan's repertoire of insults was better than Jeff's, and Sara decided she was glad Jeff wasn't so glib in this kind of contest.

She and Jeff continued to do homework together the rest of the week, followed by short walks afterward. But on the way home from the bus stop on Friday, Jeff grumbled, "I won't even be able to study with you tonight. Dad wants me in bed early since we get up so early in the morning." He looked tired already and he hadn't spent the day fishing yet. "But I'll call you tomorrow night," he promised, with a look at Sara that made her go weak. He really was going to miss her!

"Okay," she said brightly, trying to make him feel better. "I understand there are times when a guy has things to do. I'm not a fisherman's daughter for nothing."

"Yeah," Jeff said, but it didn't sound like she'd cheered him up any. "It must be nice to have such a wonderful attitude all the time." He smiled to take the sting out of his slightly sarcastic words.

They kissed good-bye at her doorstep and Sara went inside, feeling melancholy.

She wondered how to spend the evening, since she couldn't look forward to time with Jeff. She realized she ought to call Susy and see if she wanted to come over. Since things with Jeff had gotten rolling, she'd been really ignoring Susy. Sara felt a twinge of guilt as she thought about how they used to get together constantly before Jeff had asked her out. And now she'd been a real creep, almost forgetting Susy existed. Part of it was due, Sara knew, to the way Susy had started acting. She always seemed to be nit-picking and complaining about her own lack of social life. Susy wasn't the easiest friend a girl could have, but she was just about the only one Sara had on the island. And in view of that, Sara resolved to call her after dinner.

The call turned out to be a surprise. Susy was busy. She already had plans to go out with three other girls to the same movie Sara had seen with Jeff the week before.

"Gosh, Sara, I would have asked you, but . . ." Susy did sound sorry. She even added, "You could still go with us. We could squeeze you in the backseat."

"No, it's okay," Sara protested. "I've already seen that movie. It was okay but I wouldn't want to see it again." Good grief! Now *she* sounded snotty. "I mean, you'll probably enjoy it, but . . ." How did you get out of a mess like this?

"Yeah, I know what you mean," Susy said. "It's not supposed to be the greatest movie, but at least it's something to do." There was a pause. "Uh, so what are you going to do, then?"

Sara thought over her options. It was depressing. There was homework, television, or she could mend some things. "I guess I'll fix that pink blouse," she said finally, thinking to herself: Wow! How exciting could it get?

"The pink one?" Susy asked, surprised. "But I thought

you said it was too tight. You were going to throw it away and buy a new one."

Sara frowned. That was a sore subject. The night before, when she'd actually proposed that plan to her mother, expecting full agreement, she'd been shocked when her mother said a little testily, "Sara, we don't have a money tree outside. Can't you cut the long sleeves down to make them short ones and move the buttons over a little?" The bottom line seemed to be that at the moment they couldn't afford even a new blouse. That was one more evidence of the rotten fishing Sara was trying to convince herself was going to end soon.

"Uh, no, not yet. There's still a lot of wear in it." She sounded downright defensive, and Susy was taken aback.

"Oh, well, uh . . . Hey, I understand. Even though my dad's not a fisherman, I know things are a little tight right now with the families of men who are."

Sara wished everyone would quit talking about that subject.

"Yeah, well, that's not the reason I'm fixing the blouse," she claimed, mentally hitting herself for lying.

"Oh. So have fun," Susy replied lamely.

They hung up after a couple more difficult moments during which neither girl seemed to know what to say to the other. Sara couldn't figure out if she was disappointed or relieved that she wasn't going to be with Susy tonight.

She caught a glimpse of herself in the dresser mirror and frowned. The pink blouse. Last year it had been her favorite. But that was before she grew . . . out— not up! The thought of moving the buttons over to give her more room was ridiculous. There would never be enough room.

She flopped down on her bed to daydream about Jeff. What did he think of her figure? Did he like it? Or did he even notice it? Well, he probably did notice it. Guys at school always seemed to notice that kind of stuff. Sara recalled an incident that happened shortly after Jackie had moved to North Carolina. Sara and Susy had been standing by their lockers when Jackie walked by. A couple of guys across the hall had nudged each other. One had said, "Mmm-hmm! Even her curves have curves." The other had whistled and pretended to follow after Jackie, but the first guy had held him back by his belt.

Susy had slammed her locker and muttered, "Why do guys always notice a girl's body, but never care about her brains?"

"Maybe they don't think we have brains," had been Sara's caustic reply.

But that didn't apply to Jeff, did it? He hadn't asked her out just because her figure was okay, had he? He did appreciate that she had a mind, didn't he?

She rolled over onto her stomach and tucked her chin into one palm. There was definitely something that needed working on in this big romance with Jeff. And that was communication. It seemed that Jeff did a lot of talking and she did a lot of listening, but never about anything important. She didn't know how he felt about a lot of things besides college and fishing. The next time she and Jeff spoke with each other, Sara resolved, she'd put "operation heart-talk" into action.

# 8

The next time they spoke was the following evening, when Jeff called her. "Hi, Sara, it's me, Jeff." Even before he said, "Man! Am I beat!" she could tell from his voice he was exhausted. Did you try to get a guy to open up about his deepest feelings when he was so tired his speech almost sounded slurred?

"Hi. Uh . . . how'd it go?" Brother! What a jerky question. It was obvious how it went.

"Just terrific. I think we actually caught enough fish to pay for the diesel fuel we used to get out there in the first place." Jeff paused a minute, groaning. "My back aches, my feet ache, I've got windburn on all the exposed parts of my body, and I think my nose froze off and fell overboard, but I'm not sure because I can't feel anything with my fingers anymore."

Sara wasn't sure if she was supposed to laugh. That hadn't exactly sounded like a joke.

"I wanted to come over tonight and see you, but I'm bushed. I think I'll hit the sack. But I'll be over tomorrow. Okay?"

"Sure. I understand." Sara forced herself not to sound disappointed. Seeing Jeff tonight would have been great. She'd spent the whole day waiting for this phone call, and it wasn't turning out the way she'd planned.

"Good," Jeff sighed. "See you tomorrow. Good night."

"Good night." Right after she spoke she heard the sound of the click as he hung up. It was as if he couldn't wait to get off the phone and hit the mattress.

Suddenly a picture popped into her mind. It was of her dad the way he always came in after a day of fishing. Whether it had been successful or not, he always looked like all he wanted in the world was to drop into the nearest chair and never get up. Oh, there were those times when a good catch that day had put a big smile of satisfaction on his weary face. But lately there hadn't been too many of those. In fact, these days he just dragged in, flopped onto the couch, and only moved to go to the dinner table. She had never really thought about that before. She guessed when it was your father, you didn't pay much attention to how he looked or acted when he came home from work. It was all a part of everyday life.

But was that how it would be for Jeff? If he became a fisherman like his dad and Sara's, would that be a part of his life—exhaustion at night so total that he could hardly keep up his end of a conversation? Was that the way Sara wanted it if they ever got married? Did she *really* want the same life she saw her mother having? Somehow she'd always thought she did.

She left the parlor, where she'd been talking on the phone with Jeff, and glanced through the doorway to the living room, where the family was watching TV. She paused, looking at her father. His legs were straight out in front of him and his whole body looked like it was melting into the upholstery of his favorite chair. He looks so old! she thought in shock.

Sara moved on down the hall toward the kitchen. But Jeff wasn't old. He was young and strong. His problem wasn't really a physical one. It was the way he thought. She poured herself a glass of milk, thinking: Jeff's got an attitude problem. He was always thinking about what he didn't like about fishing instead of what he did like. Taking one of the brownies she'd made that day, Sara sat down at the kitchen table, eating it absentmindedly.

Her grandmother had a favorite song about how you had to concentrate on the positive and not think about the negative. And the positive things about fishing were great. Sara loved being out on a boat. There was nothing like the sound of the water, the gulls, the feel of the salt air blowing through your hair. There were a lot of things Jeff could think about instead of grousing about the hard work and temporary lack of reward. If he'd just change his attitude he'd be happy. Sara decided it was up to her to help Jeff do that. And she'd start tomorrow when he came over.

She rose to throw away her napkin and wash her glass out in the sink. She'd just skip upstairs and see if she could dredge up something to wear tomorrow that would take Jeff's mind off the bad things and put him into a better frame of mind.

She had it all figured out the next day. First she would get Jeff out of the house for a walk. March had ended, and anytime now spring would make its first showing. Buds on trees and bushes were growing fatter. The sky was that intensely clear blue that made Sara feel she could see as far away as the next galaxy. A day such as this shouldn't be spent cooped up in the house. She'd steer Jeff down to the dock and maybe talk about fishing. It would be a natural thing to talk about with her dad's boat sitting there on the water right next to them. Confidence in her plan gave Sara's step a bounce when she went to let Jeff in.

But she learned her first lesson about making plans that included boys. You could plan to your heart's content, but a boy could blow them in seconds flat.

"Let's take Shep for a walk," Sara suggested before Jeff got his coat off.

"Okay."

So far, so good, Sara thought gleefully as she went to tell her parents where she was going and to collect the dog.

But from there on, Sara lost control of the situation. As soon as they got out the front door and Sara would have turned toward the water and the dock, Jeff took her hand and headed in the opposite direction.

"But . . ." She stopped in her tracks, glancing toward the dock. "I thought we could go down by the water."

"No way!" Jeff said firmly. "I've had it up to here with water for a while." He made a slicing motion in front of his throat with his free hand and began walking determinedly toward the open field. "I'm going to see if I can find the exact geographical center of this island and hope I can't even smell the ocean."

Oh-oh! Sara thought. This didn't look promising for a big heart-to-heart-talk scene. Momentarily she thought of trying to stick to her guns and head for the dock, but decided to give up in favor of Jeff's getting his way. He'd be easier to talk to if they didn't start out the day arguing over a silly thing like their destination. Besides, Shep was halfway to the field by now. Jeff followed the dog, which was at a flat-out gallop. That dog was so familiar with their routine by now, he didn't need anyone to tell him where they were going.

Jeff didn't seem to be in a particularly gabby mood today, either; he just walked along on his long legs without saying anything. Sara couldn't have talked if she wanted to. She was practically trotting to keep up with him. She was fast running out of breath and finally stopped short, crying, "Hey! Where's the fire?"

"Huh?" Jeff looked out of it. He stared at her a moment before he figured out what she meant. Then he smiled and scooped her up in his arms. "Sorry," he said, and started walking, carrying her.

"Jeff!" she cried, even more breathless than before. What had gotten into him?

"Sara!" he mocked with a grin.

"Jeff! What's with this?" Her face was inches from his and she could feel it turning red. Quickly she looked away from him and concentrated on the field as Jeff crossed the road, still toting her.

"Well, it seems you're a little slow today, and there's something I've been wanting to do for over twenty-four hours. And if I want to do it as soon as possible, I guess I'll just have to carry you."

"Oh? What is it?" Curiosity made Sara turn back to Jeff. His eyes twinkled as he let her feet drop, but kept his arms around her.

"This," he said right before he kissed her.

After a long while Sara said, "Ohhhh."

They started walking again, aimlessly wandering through the field. Shep's curvy, bushy tail was their guide as he explored all the interesting attractions of the field. They sidestepped the bushes and tall prickly weeds, avoided the marshy spots and stepped on the firmer ones, until they'd gotten completely out of sight of civilization. Despite Jeff's plans, they were within sight of an inlet and the salty tang of ocean air was always with them. But if it bothered him, he didn't say.

He did look a lot happier than when he'd first come

to the house, Sara observed. She wondered what had caused his initial bad mood.

Jeff pulled a piece of paper from his pocket and offered it to her. "Read this and tell me what you think. It's that editorial. I polished it up Friday night. I'll turn it in tomorrow."

Sara took it. "You mean you were writing for the newspaper instead of doing the homework you told me your dad expected you to do?" she blurted out. Disappointment and disbelief rang out in her voice. She wasn't sure why she felt hurt; she just did.

Jeff frowned and stuffed his hands in his pockets. "No—*after* I did the homework." He looked at Sara as if she were a stranger he couldn't figure out.

She was instantly sorry she'd shot off her big mouth. She had to stop being so sensitive about his newspaper work. When she read Jeff's piece, she didn't have to fake interest, though, because as soon as she started on it she was engrossed. He'd used a humorous touch but there was almost a biting satirical undercurrent to his observations. He'd really let the board members have it. She raised her eyes to his when she was done.

"This is really something! You made some good points, but . . . uh . . . don't you think you're going to blow some people's minds with this?"

He shrugged but looked extremely pleased with himself. "Maybe, but good journalism is supposed to move people. It shouldn't just take up space on a page." He looked down at the paper she still had in her hand. "You really think it's good?" He actually sounded like her opinion was important to him.

Don't blow this, Sara cautioned herself. "Jeff, I'm not too up on literary stuff, you know. But it seems to me like this is really well written. I mean, it doesn't sound at all like a seventeen-year-old wrote it."

His smile broadened. He didn't say anything, but took

the paper from her, stuffed it in his pocket, and flung one arm around her. They started walking again.

Under their feet, down below the matted tangle of dried grasses and weeds, tiny new shoots of grass, a tender green, struggled valiantly to reach the sun. Spring's earliest sign.

They walked side by side for a while, talking aimlessly about school.

"Is Mrs. Bruebaker still assigning those weird essays in Soc?" Jeff asked, picking up a stick to throw it for Shep.

"Oh, yeah. In fact she just gave us one. Listen to this." Sara began reciting in a pseudo-serious voice, "You are a superior being. You want to get a message to lesser beings who are experiencing grave troubles. You have the answer to their problems. How would you go about it?" She laughed and rammed her hands into the pockets of her jeans.

"So what did you write?" Jeff eyed her with evident interest.

"Oh, well, I thought and thought. And you know? I thought how that sounded just like God and humans. We were supposed to identify who the superior being and the inferior ones are, and explain the method of communication. I know God had communicated with man with the Bible. But the only way I could remember that he did it was when he carved out the Ten Commandments in stone. I thought that was too primitive for modern man." Sara stopped and picked up a stick for Shep, tossing it as far as she could.

"Yeah?" Jeff prompted, wanting her to continue.

"Well, something Jackie said a while back about excuses for not getting work done—you know, the computer was down?"

"Yeah."

"So I decided that I'd be God trying to get in touch

with man. So what I'd do is make every single computer on the planet go down—just stop working. I'd have it that way for about an hour to get everyone's attention. After that I'd send a message at the same time to all the computers in whatever language was used by the programmers. They'd all try to find out who was doing it, but since *all* the computers, those in government, business, homes, even the UN, would be printing out the same message, they'd have to realize that no human could possibly connect up to all the computers all over the world at the same time. It'd be impossible. Then when I told them it was God doing that, they might believe it." She turned toward Jeff and said with a shrug, "So that's what I wrote."

Jeff stopped walking and looked at Sara with a new expression. "Hey! Not bad. I never knew you were such a deep thinker."

Sara put her hands on her hips. "What did you think I was? An ignoramus?" she demanded, half-joking and half-serious.

Jeff grabbed her hand and squeezed it. "No, no, Sara! I guess I just thought of you as . . . well, kind of satisfied with life as you found it. You know, like you really didn't think seriously about the future. That you were content with things . . ." His voice trailed off as he realized his words weren't particularly flattering.

Sara's face reflected her dislike for the way he portrayed her.

"What are your plans for the future, after you graduate?" he asked softly. He held on to her hand and sat down on a hummock, pulling her down to sit on his lap. "Tell me about them."

Sitting on a boy's lap wasn't exactly the position Sara would have chosen for discussing life's dreams and their pursuit. But she had to try. But then she thought: How could her little dreams of marrying and raising kids, of living on the island—and nothing more—ever compare with Jeff's plan of being a sportswriter or newspaper reporter? She'd really sound like a simpleton then. But that was all she'd ever considered.

"Well?" Jeff asked. "Are you going to tell me, or is it a state secret?"

Sara turned away and found her tone of voice when she spoke sounded defensive. "I expect I'll get married someday, and naturally there'd be a family."

"That's all?" Jeff asked incredulously.

"I like little kids!" she flared, turning back to him. She attempted to get up off his lap, but Jeff held her down.

"Calm down," he said placatingly. "There's nothing wrong with wanting a family." His tone was calm, reasonable, as he went on. "But there should be something first. Before that you ought to do something else. Like college. Haven't your folks expressed an interest in your going to college or something?" But before she had a chance to answer, he frowned and answered his own question. "No, of course they wouldn't." He looked disgusted, making Sara automatically feel defensive.

"What do you mean by saying that?"

He looked instantly apologetic. "I only meant that knowing your dad, college is probably out of the question for you. He isn't too great on girls expanding their minds, is he?"

Sara didn't know how to answer that without making her father look like a chauvinist. But she had to admit to herself that Jeff's assessment of her father was correct.

"Hey, look, I don't want to get into an argument with you," Jeff said softly. "So let's not talk." His lips touched hers, and found no argument there.

They lay back on the ground and hugged each other. Shep bounded up and started licking them in the face. They laughed, trying to push him away. Finally they had to stand up and start walking again, tossing Shep his stick to keep him happy. Jeff looked relaxed and at ease. Now, while he was in a good mood, Sara thought, talk to him about fishing.

"So . . . uh . . . tell me about yesterday."

"Yesterday?" Jeff's face looked blank.

"Yeah, you know, about fishing. Was it really all that bad? Weren't there any good things that happened?"

"Are you kidding? What could happen that's good? That motor broke down again and I had to lie out on the deck on a smelly old wool blanket and help Dad fix it. Meanwhile, a million fish could have come by but we wouldn't have been able to do anything about it. 'Course, a million fish *didn't* come by."

"Oh." Sara's voice sounded small. She had to think of something positive quickly. "Well, wasn't it fun just to be out on the ocean again?"

"Not when fuel costs so much," Jeff retorted.

"Uh, yeah. Well . . ." Sara felt exactly like an ignoramus now. She tripped over a clump of grass, her face burning. Jeff hauled her back up onto her feet with the words, "Twinkle Toes does it again. First day with new feet?" using an old nickname he used to have for her during her awkward stage.

She socked him, and felt intense satisfaction giving vent to her frustration. He just laughed and followed the bouncing canine tail. Sara noticed they were going in an arc that would have them back at her house soon. She had to talk fast. Lately she'd noticed as soon as Shep saw the house he made a beeline for it and there was no calling him back.

"Well, I guess after graduation, if you get your own boat you can make sure it's in good shape mechanically, and maybe that kind of thing won't happen to you."

Jeff's mouth turned down at the corners. He stopped and turned Sara so she faced him. "Sara, after graduation

I'm not going to get my own boat. Haven't you been paying attention? I don't want to be a fisherman. *Ever.*" He spoke clearly, as if he were talking to someone who had to read his lips.

Sara's whole body went still. Here it was, out in the open. No more pretending. "Not ever?" she asked in a shaky voice.

"No, not ever. I don't think I'd be happy staying in the rut I was born in." He waved an arm, pointing to the world around them. "Sara, look around you. What do you see? Jackie says we're in a time warp here, and she's right. My parents are happy; I'll give them that. But the kind of life that's right for them is from the last century. This is the eighties. I want to grow with this century, not be stuck back in time doing something that can't keep up with life in the present. Dad and Mom can't see any other kind of life but fishing, eating, sleeping, and raising kids.

"Don't get me wrong; I love my parents. I really appreciate the sacrifices they've made for us boys. But I want something better, a bigger piece of the pie."

This was one of the longest speeches he'd ever given, and Sara thought a little dryly: Well, I wanted a heart-to-heart talk!

Jeff paced away a few feet and then turned toward her. "This place is okay. No—it's better than okay. It's beautiful. But for me it's not enough. I'm really crazy about writing for the paper. I can see myself someday with a byline in all kinds of papers. National circulation. I have dreams like that." His face had been animated, but suddenly it clouded, and he slammed a fist into his palm. "But it looks like I can't have my dreams. Unless I do something about them—soon!" He walked over to Sara, a fierce intensity in his gaze as he held her face in his hands. "Sara, I like to dream as much as the next guy, but there comes a time when dreams have

to become reality or there's no point in dreaming anymore. And without dreams, a life isn't living, it's just
existing."

Sara was a little confused. "Jeff, I'm not sure what
you're trying to say."

"Sara," he sighed, taking a deep breath before explaining patiently, "What I'm trying to say is, I have to tell
my dad that I don't want to join him on the boat after
graduation and have that be the end of my education.
Even though that's next year, he's going to need time
to get used to it. If he ever does," he muttered under
his breath. Sara was beginning to get the picture. When
Jeff finally told his parents about his "dreams," they
were going to flip out. She felt sorry for them. For Jeff.
And for herself.

"Oh. So . . . uh . . . what exactly are you going to
do instead?"

"See if I can get into college for journalism. Then
get a job on a paper somewhere."

*Somewhere.* But not *here.*

Sara hurt all over. Her eyes burned, her throat ached,
and all she wanted to do was go home and never see
Jeff again. What would be the point? Why fall head over
heels in love with a guy who was going to disappear
out of your life in a year and a half? Save yourself the
heartache by cutting it off now, she told herself. But
she couldn't do it. She just didn't have the guts. She'd
take Jeff for a year, a month, a day. Whatever she was
allowed. And when the end came? Well . . . she didn't
want to think about that now. I'm a regular Scarlett
O'Hara, she thought.

Sara started walking toward her house, expecting Jeff
to follow. "Well, I hope you get what you want," she
choked out. If she tried to say anything more, she'd
be bawling. Her steps got quicker and it was Jeff's turn
to hurry to catch up.

He didn't say anything. Out of the corner of her eye she saw him glancing at her from time to time, but neither spoke all the way home. Sara didn't know what was going through his mind, but it was pretty clear to her that Jeff had his whole future all planned out. And he hadn't said a thing about her being in it, so what more was there to say?

By the time they reached Sara's front door she was out of breath. Jeff stood there looking at her with a puzzled expression.

"Do you want to come in?" she asked stiffly. No matter how hard she tried, she couldn't make herself loosen up and act natural.

Jeff reached out and took her hand. "Sara? What's bugging you?" he asked softly.

"Nothing." She shrugged. He really didn't have a clue! she thought in exasperation.

"Come on. Give me more credit. Ever since we started talking about me working for a newspaper, you've acted uptight. What's wrong? Don't you really think I could make it?"

"That's not it. If you really want it, you'll get it. It's just that I . . . um . . . I'm kind of tired today." It wasn't really a lie; she *was* tired. And exhausted, depressed, resentful, angry—she could come up with a million emotions right now to explain her attitude. But if you got right down to it, the basic problem was, if Jeff would only open up and tell her how he felt about *her*, then maybe the future wouldn't look so bleak.

He looked down at her a couple more seconds, then kissed her on the forehead. "Well, if you're tired, why don't you go get some rest? See you tomorrow?"

"Yeah," she answered huskily. Pain was squeezing her chest so tightly she felt suffocated. Quickly she turned and went inside, holding the door open for Shep, who bounded through.

The dog trotted into the living room and lay down at his master's feet. His tongue hung out and his chest heaved. Sara's father patted the dog on his side.

"Boy, Shep sure is getting a lot of walks lately," he quipped, with a sidelong glance at Sara, who hovered by the door.

"Right," Gram piped in. "And even when he doesn't *want* to go for a walk." Her son chuckled and Sara's mother, who sat next to him on the couch, reached down and scratched the dog behind the ears.

"Poor Shep," she said so softly Sara almost didn't hear. "What he'll endure for love."

Sara moved out of the doorway hastily and mounted the stairs to her room. It looked like she and Jeff hadn't been fooling anyone by claiming they were just taking the dog for walks. But was it like her mother said? Was it really love? On her part, yes. But Sara didn't think love played much of a part in Jeff's life. Except for his obvious infatuation with being a newspaper reporter.

She slumped on her bed, staring vacantly in front of her. Then her gaze focused on the pink blouse. She'd dragged it out of the closet the night before and thrown it over her desk chair, intending to get serious about altering it. That blouse is just like my dreams, she thought. Nothing fit anymore. And like the blouse, she had three choices. Change her dreams to fit the new situation; throw them out and start all over again with a new guy in them; or hang on to the old ones even though they weren't right anymore. Deep down in her heart Sara knew which one she wanted, and it hurt to know it was the one that looked like it would never work out. What was it Jeff had said about dreams? There comes a time when dreams have to become reality or there's no point in dreaming anymore. Had the time come for her to stop dreaming?

# 9

For the rest of the day Sara felt so depressed she thought she'd rather die. By the time the evening meal was over, she needed to talk to someone so badly she felt ready to burst. Throwing on a hat and coat, she told her mom, "I'm going to see Susy."

"Come back before dark," her mother said with a glance at the clock.

She walked along in the cool evening air, wondering when spring would finally come. She needed spring, but this April seemed to be holding one last cold spell up its sleeve. She shivered a little and turned down Susy's lane. It was graveled with crushed shells and her feet made a crunching sound as she walked. She wasn't exactly sure what she was going to say to Susy, but she really needed to talk to someone.

Susy's mother seemed quite surprised to see her.

"Why, Sara! Did Susy know you were coming over?" Mrs. Pitcher looked uncomfortable.

"Uh . . . no." Sara stepped into the house, preparing to unbutton her coat, but she never had to.

"Oh. Well, she's not here."

"She's not?" Sara was dumbfounded.

"No. I'm sorry. She's out with Marsha and Trish. They went over to Nancy's to practice a new dance step or something. I'm expecting her back around ten." Susy's mother sounded so apologetic Sara immediately tried to reassure her.

"Oh, don't worry about it. I probably should have called. Just tell her I came by."

Sara walked home slowly. She felt worse than ever. Susy seemed to be filling the empty spot Sara had left very nicely. It sure looked like she didn't need Sara's friendship anymore. She felt abandoned, like no one really needed her. Susy had new friends. Jeff had plans for his future that didn't include her. Sara felt if she died on the way home, no one would miss her for long.

She picked up a twig and flung it across the road. I have to stop this, she thought. When a person actually starts thinking about her own death, she'd better get straightened out. Sara knew it wasn't like her. When she got home she was going to talk to Gram. Gram could always put things into perspective.

She found Gram in the kitchen making herself a cup of tea. Joy was sitting at the table coloring and drinking some hot chocolate. It would be her bedtime soon.

"Gram, can I talk to you after Joy goes to bed?" Sara asked as she took down a cup for herself.

"Of course." Gram smiled but didn't ask about what. She seemed to have a sixth sense about things like that.

"How come everyone is always saying how they're gonna do stuff *after* I go to bed?" Joy asked in an exasperated little voice.

Sara laughed and went to kiss her sister on the top of her head. "That's not true. It only seems like that. Besides, you go to bed earlier than anyone else, so of course the rest of us do things after you're in bed."

Joy looked at Sara with an expression that showed she wasn't totally convinced. "Why do I always hafta go to bed earlier?"

"Because you need your beauty sleep," Gram told her, and started collecting the crayons that were spread all over.

"Huh?" Joy looked confused.

Sara smiled as Gram led Joy upstairs, explaining "beauty sleep" to her. A few minutes later Gram was back, pulling out a chair to sit with Sara at the kitchen table.

"Now, what's troubling my favorite sixteen-year-old granddaughter?"

Sara smiled. "Your *only* sixteen-year-old granddaughter," she teased, then sobered as she tried to think how to put into words what was bothering her. She wrapped her hands around the mug of hot cocoa and looked down at the table in embarrassment.

"Let me guess," Gram said. "It's about a certain boy with dark brown hair and Atlantic-blue eyes?"

"Gram!" Sara exclaimed. "I didn't think anyone noticed his eyes." She looked at her grandmother in astonishment.

Gram smiled like the Mona Lisa. "Did you think only people in love noticed things like that?" she chided.

"Yes . . . I mean, no . . ." Sara floundered, then took a deep breath. "Yes," she sighed. "I am bothered about things with Jeff." She launched into an explanation about his work on the *Scuttlebutt* and his plans for college. She didn't leave anything out and was surprised that Gram didn't react particularly to the news that Jeff wasn't interested in staying on the island and fishing. "Gram, I'm scared. If he goes away to college, I'll hardly ever see him. He'll find someone new at college and I'll lose him." She flushed. "That is, if I ever get him."

"You don't think you've got him now?"

"I don't know," Sara moaned, and fidgeted with her mug. "He . . . he never says anything about how he feels about me. I don't know if he really cares about me or what."

"But you're sure you're in love with him and it's not just infatuation?" Gram prompted in her no-nonsense manner.

"Oh, no! I really love him," Sara insisted.

"You know, Sara, what you're feeling could be either. And whatever Jeff's feeling could be either. Maybe he's the smart one and doesn't want to say anything until he's sure.

"Love's a funny thing. Infatuation starts quick and ends just as quick. But love's got to simmer on the back burner awhile. It takes time, Sara, to make sure which it is. So be patient with him, honey. Give him time, too." Gram patted Sara's hand and stood up, taking her empty cup to the sink. "If it's love, you'll find out soon enough. And all the waiting will have been worth it."

Sara sat there for a while after Gram left, reflecting on her words. That was Gram for you. She had this incredible knack for starting the wheels in your head turning.

During the night Sara came to a conclusion. Somehow, while she slept, her brain had still been thinking about the problem with Jeff and made a decision. When she woke, she got up with the idea full-blown in her head. She'd keep her mouth shut about fishing and show interest in the newspaper whenever he talked about it. A surefire way to cool a guy's interest in you was to show a lack of enthusiasm for the things he was crazy about.

So that was what she'd do. She wouldn't try to get Jeff talking about fishing right now. That was a dangerous subject. She'd concentrate instead on safe ones. Give it time, Gram had said.

And she did.

All the rest of April Sara let Jeff set the pace for their relationship. They went out every Friday night, either to a movie or just to the Pizza Inn. A couple of times Mike and Peg joined them and there was a lot of laughing. Sara noticed that Jeff didn't act weird those times like he'd done the first night when Sara had met them. If he had been jealous that time, maybe he was so sure of her now he didn't feel the same way, she mused.

When the two families got together in April for their monthly dinner, Sara realized Jeff still hadn't told his father about wanting to go to college. They were sitting around the dinner table, tucking into the fried-chicken-and-mashed-potato dinner. As usual, the fathers took over all conversation.

"I told Jeff when he graduates I plan on taking out a loan and getting a new boat. That old bucket is really ready for a major overhaul. With two of us working, we should be able to earn enough to pay off the loan. Hate to do it, but I can't see Jeff making his living on an old wreck." Jim chuckled.

Sara, sitting beside Jeff, slid him a questioning look while she listened to his father. He caught her eye and looked away quickly. His tan deepened and she realized he was blushing. Had he been putting off telling his parents for some reason? Was he that afraid of their reactions? Or was he all talk? Maybe he wanted college and told the kids at school about it, but knew deep in his heart that there was no way he could ever really go. Did he realize that he'd have to join his father after school whether he wanted to or not? If that were true, then he hadn't been entirely honest with the kids or

Sara. Sara suddenly lost her appetite. That could only mean one thing. What Jeff felt for her couldn't be love. If you loved a person, you were totally honest with him or her.

Jeff and Sara had promised in a moment of weakness to play Monopoly with his brothers after dinner, so there wasn't time to talk about it then. When Monday morning came and they were on the bus, Jeff seemed to be in such a cheerful mood she didn't want to ruin it. So in keeping with her decision not to talk about dangerous subjects, Sara kept quiet.

When the *Scuttlebutt* came out in April, Jeff's editorial, slightly toned down by the paper's adviser, appeared in it. He was the talk of the school. Kids stopped him in the halls to compliment him or express surprise that he'd been allowed to write so forcefully on the subject.

"Thought you wanted to be a sportswriter," one senior said on the bus. "Looks like you ought to be a muckraker." Jeff beamed all the way home.

One of the board members who hadn't been in favor of the cutbacks for the coming year actually called Jeff up to express his appreciation. But he told him that despite the accuracy of Jeff's points, the fact remained that the budget just didn't allow room for the sports expenditures. Unless money was found from somewhere else, the vote would have to stand.

While Jeff was getting all this attention, Sara firmly trampled down her feelings and smiled widely at him. When the English teacher made his editorial required reading for the class, she realized he had a real talent that would go to waste if he had to spend his life fishing. She wondered if he'd ever found out about scholarships, but was afraid to ask. She convinced herself that if Jeff had found out anything good about that, he'd have told her.

Spring finally came. The forsythia and pussywillows

opened up; Mrs. Wilson's daffodils, crocuses, and grape hyacinths all bobbed their many-colored heads in the April breeze. It was a wetter month than usual, which curtailed Sara and Jeff's walks in the field a little and they had to spend more time inside. But the times they were free to go out were wonderful. Sometimes they just walked holding hands and sometimes they talked about school, their families, or friends. But whenever Jeff started complaining about fishing, which was almost every time they were together, Sara got uptight. She finally discovered a great way to stop Jeff's griping. She kissed him. And then there were several moments of peace and quiet.

The problem with that, though, was that a couple of times things got really hot and heavy. When that happened, Sara was scared in every part of her body. Jeff would take her hand, pull her to her feet, and simply hold her until their hearts stopped beating so fast. Then they'd walk back to the house, slowly so they could get their breath back. Sara was glad he never wanted her to give more than she was prepared to. It showed he respected her, and he must care for her. She decided after one of those heavy sessions as they were ambling home that he probably even loved her, but he must be one of those men she'd heard her mother talking about to a friend once.

"Some men just can't say the words 'I love you.' They figure you know they do by their actions. They show it, but can't get the words out."

Sara decided that was the way her father was. He was affectionate, but never in her life had she heard him tell her mom he loved her. So she figured Jeff was the same kind of man; he couldn't get the words out. But when he showed her consideration she knew it was because he cared for her a lot. She'd love to hear the words, but she'd settle for actions.

The fact that there was still a tiny bit of doubt in her mind made Sara a little unhappy. She wished she had the courage to ask Jeff exactly what he felt for her, but she didn't. And she was guilty of the same thing: she never actually told Jeff how she felt about him either.

Things between them just coasted along for a while, like a ship on calm water, until one night something happened that really rocked the boat. It was mid-May, and Sara had noticed that Jeff seemed to be preoccupied a lot lately. But she figured he was as busy as she was gearing up for final exams and the end of school. It seemed like all the teachers suddenly remembered a mess of projects they'd wanted to assign the kids during the year, and were cramming them all into the last month of school.

Jeff had promised to come over after dinner one night and help Sara study her math, but when he came, Sara took one look at his face and knew something was terribly wrong. Without saying a thing, she led him to the kitchen and got them Cokes and a plate of chocolate-chip cookies. When Jeff didn't touch the cookies, which were his favorite, she knew something really serious was coming down. He opened his books, but she noticed that one was upside down. As she was trying to decide if she should say anything or pretend everything was normal, Jeff slammed a notebook shut, making her jump.

"What's the matter?" she croaked.

Jeff scowled, then leaned forward on his elbows. "Sara, I told my folks about wanting to go to college."

"Oh." So that was it. "What did they say?"

"Just what I expected. 'We haven't any money for college.'"

"What about a scholarship?"

"Mr. Carter checked for me, and he found I was qualified for a couple, but there's a lot of competition for them and even if I could get one, I'd still need big bucks of my own. I'd have to come home every weekend to help Dad out, and that would mean extra transportation costs. Dad just can't do the work alone much longer. Together we'd bring in more fish than he can by himself." Jeff got up and began pacing around the kitchen. "He told me if I want to go to college I'll have to save all the money I make helping him right now because he can't spare a dime. The old man's unreasonable!" Sara noticed the use of the term "old man"—another Jackie-ism, she thought. "If I save all my bread for college, that'll leave none for taking you out!"

Sara tried to placate him. "But that's okay. We can just do things that don't cost anything."

He gave her a look that made her wish she'd kept her mouth shut. "Sure. We could do that. But we'd really miss going out with the crowd and doing things in town. The way Dad's talking, I'm going to be chained to that boat every weekend from now on. Maybe we can keep in touch with each other by phone!" he snapped sarcastically.

Things were definitely getting bad here. Sara had to think of a way to defuse it. But Jeff went on, still pacing the floor. One fist was balled up in his pocket, and he gestured angrily with the other hand. Sara had never seen him so upset.

"Dad can't understand why I wouldn't be happy being a fisherman like he is. You should have heard him tonight. 'There's food on the table and clothes on you kids' backs. What more do you want?' Man! I'd like to have told him. But it wouldn't have done any good. We're not just from different generations, we're from different worlds. He's happy with a TV and a beer. But the house is shabby. Mom's always wanting some new curtains to brighten up the place, or maybe a new rug. And all he says is, 'The old ones are fine.' But the real reason is there's never any money for those things. So Mom clams up, but I know she gets depressed."

Jeff stopped at the table to gulp down some of his

Coke, as if his speech had dried out his mouth. Sara was beginning to feel disturbed. That last thing he'd talked about sounded too familiar for comfort. She could almost hear her parents carrying on the same conversation. Change the names and the faces, but the circumstances were the same. Her mother's biggest complaint was that their furniture, while neat and in fairly good condition considering its age, was so blah. It didn't really come under any headings like colonial, modern, or anything else. Her mother called it "early serviceable." And the kitchen was a study in antiquity too. All the appliances were ancient, the floor was worn, and the painted moldings around the doors were a scratch-and-dent exhibition. This place is shabby too, she thought as she let herself look around.

Jeff caught the movement of her eyes. It was as if he knew what she was thinking. He nodded at her. "Yeah, look around you. This place is okay, but it sure isn't the Taj Mahal either."

Sara quickly looked down at her homework. She felt a little hurt. It was one thing to complain about your own house, but it was quite another to point out the defects of someone else's.

"I just live here, I'm not the decorator," she mumbled. If Jeff heard her, he didn't react.

"Why did our fathers have to choose fishing?" he stormed, and Sara's head snapped up. "Didn't either of them have enough brains to see it's no way to make a living?"

He looked at Sara, pointing with his arm toward the front of the house. "I always thought your dad was smart. So why hasn't he given up fishing, moved off the island, and gotten a *real* job?"

Sara felt like a steam-filled kettle, getting hotter and hotter.

"I mean, look at you and Joy. You girls have always

had clothes on your backs too, but nothing special. It's just like Jackie said—"

Sara couldn't stand any more. She stood up so fast her chair fell over backward. The action brought Jeff's tirade to a halt mid-sentence as he stood there, his mouth still open.

"Who do you think you are, criticizing my dad?" Sara challenged. "You can pick on fishing, you can pick on your dad, and you can even pick on me. But don't talk about my dad."

"Sara, I—"

She wasn't about to be stopped now. She cut him off with a wave of her hand. "Okay, so you're going to have to work a little harder to get money for that college you seem to want so badly. But that doesn't give you the right to find fault with my father's chosen occupation. He works hard, that's true. Fishing *is* hard work, but it's all Dad's ever known. Gramps was a fisherman; he trained Dad to follow in his footsteps. Fishing has been a part of our family for generations. It's part of our heritage. And it's an important part of the world, too. There are hungry people out there. What do you want them to do? Starve? There are poor people who fish every day just so they can get a meal once a day, and if they have a little extra, they sell it. They don't know how to do anything else, so it's a good thing they fish or they'd never make ends meet.

"And what about restaurants? Seafood's considered a special part of the menu, isn't it? Well, how would it get there without fishermen? Huh? Tell me that!"

Sara had been standing there gripping the back of her chair that she had picked up. Now she shoved it under the table so hard the pile of schoolbooks on the tabletop slid over and two of them fell onto the floor. Jeff looked from the books to Sara, not sure what to do. It seemed like he wanted to say something, but Sara was so mad by now, she could almost see red. Weeks of keeping her feelings to herself made her burst out now, and there was no stopping her.

"At least fishing is clean, honest work. You sure can't say that about newspaper snoops." Jeff's eyebrows went up at the biting tone she was using. His mouth tightened and she should have taken that as a red flag of warning, but she didn't. "All reporters do is snoop around in other people's business and then write about it. They harass public figures and expose people's weaknesses and mistakes—"

"Now, just a minute! You'd better shut up before you're in over your head," Jeff warned, his face set. He stepped toward her.

Sara gasped. She felt like she had when her father spanked her as a child. Jeff had never talked to her like that before, and she resented it. "Look who's talking about being over your head. You can dish it out about an honorable profession like fishing, but you sure can't take it when it comes to your precious newspaper work." She took a step toward him and they were within three feet of each other—close enough to see the hurt and anger in each other's eyes.

"That's right—it's newspaper *work*, not *snooping*. It's hard work digging out news about things that the public has the right to know. And I'm not talking about those sleazy pulp types. I'm talking about the real newspaper reporting. How would this country have learned about things like Watergate without newspeople? Or the Bay of Pigs, or the Iranian hostages, or all the different assassinations? And it's not just things like that. There are good things reported on in papers, too—"

"Name one!" Sara demanded, her arms crossed over her chest. Sara was almost as surprised at herself as Jeff looked, but he'd hurt her and now she had an unreasonable urge to hurt back.

Jeff's mouth opened and closed. "Sara, you know I'm right!" he exploded. "What are you, living in a hole somewhere?" He stopped suddenly and looked at her hard. "You know the real issue here isn't the newspaper job. This isn't like you. You're usually so sensible. You know what I think your problem is? You don't like change. You can't stand the idea of going out and taking chances. I said once before that you're content with things the way they are. You want life to go on like it has for decades, even if that means I'd be miserable. You're selfish. Instead of resisting my dreams every chance you get, you should be supporting them. But I guess I expected too much from you. If you want to go on living in the Dark Ages along with the rest of this place, that's fine with me. Be old-fashioned! See if I care!" He threw up his hands in exasperation.

Sara stepped back as if she'd been slapped. "If that's the way you feel, then maybe you shouldn't be wasting your valuable time on an old-fashioned girl like me. Go find yourself a nice modern one." Even after the words came out she couldn't believe she'd said them.

Jeff stared at her a moment. Sara's face was flushed and she was struggling not to cry. He piled his books up roughly and swiped them off the table.

"Yeah," he muttered through his teeth. "Maybe I should. It's obvious we haven't got anything in common." He started to walk past her, paused, and planted a fast angry kiss on her lips. "Good-bye, Sara." The words rang out like gun shot. He sounded like they were never going to see each other again!

Sara stood there, shocked, and listened to every step that took him out of her house. And out of her life.

# 10

The house was totally silent. Sara couldn't even hear the television, which had been on when Jeff first arrived. That meant the whole family had heard every word! Sara felt her cheeks burning and she put her hands over them as tears finally began to fall. How could she face anyone? Without even collecting her books, Sara fled the kitchen and was halfway up the stairs before anyone in the living room stirred. Then she heard someone get up and head toward the stairs.

"Ruth, wait," Gram called. "Don't go up yet," she advised. "That poor girl needs time to weep."

Sara heard her mother's murmured reply before she shut the door to her room and flung herself across her bed. No footsteps followed her and she knew her mother had taken the advice. Good old Gram. She'd come through again. The very last thing Sara wanted to do was talk to anyone right then. Maybe not ever. Right now she just wanted to die. What was there to live for now? Jeff had walked out of her life and it was all because she'd shot off her big mouth! Why hadn't she sat there and let him carry on like always? Why had she finally snapped like that? Was it because he'd attacked her dad? That was part of it. But it also had to do with Jackie. He kept using phrases he must have picked up from her. And then to embarrass her like that by telling her she dressed poorly. Added to that were his accusations that she was selfish and resisted his dreams. That was the last straw. Maybe people in love should be honest with each other, but they should be more tactful, too!

A huge sob racked her chest, and belatedly she realized Joy was in bed. She hadn't been aware it was past her sister's bedtime. She and Jeff must have been arguing a long time. Or did it just seem like a long time? An eternity!

"Sara?" Joy's voice rose from her bed. The little girl sounded troubled. "What's the matter? Why are you crying?" Sara heard her sister throw the covers back and get out of bed. Her feet made no noise as she crossed to Sara's bed. A little hand reached out to touch Sara.

"Oh, sweetheart." Sara sighed achingly. "Go back to bed."

"But how can I? You're crying. What happened? Did someone die?"

"No! It's just . . . Jeff just . . . It's because of the way he kissed me." Good grief! Why had she blurted that out to a five-year-old?

"Huh?"

"Never mind. Go back to bed."

"But, Sara, you cried once before when he didn't kiss you, and now you're crying because he did. I don't understand."

Sara smiled in spite of her misery. Poor Joy. Life was

too hard to understand when you were as young as she was. And when your sister acted weird. But how could you explain to a little kid about a kiss that was the last one you were ever going to get?

Sara rose and took Joy back to bed, tucking her in with her Pooh bear. "Someday you'll understand it all, Joy," she told her.

And maybe someday I'll understand it all too, Sara thought as she got ready for bed. Exactly what had they been arguing about, and how come they'd been so vicious with each other? She lay there staring at the pale curtains at her window. Was it true, what Jeff said? Was she selfish? Had she been resisting his dreams? With a heart-wrenching pain Sara had to admit that to a point he'd been right. She'd constantly tried to steer the conversation away from anything even remotely connected with the newspaper, and had even begun kissing him whenever he complained about fishing. Should she have been lending him a sympathetic ear instead?

With a moan of defeat, Sara rolled over and gave up trying to sort out things in her mind. Right now she was still smarting from the hurt he'd inflicted on her by calling her selfish. Maybe in the morning she'd be up to facing everything.

When the morning came, Sara dressed for school without caring what she put on. As she went downstairs for breakfast, which she didn't want to eat, she passed by the parlor. The door was slightly ajar, and she heard voices. It was her parents and Gram.

"I don't care. I still think he's wrong."

Sara stopped. That was her dad. Who was he talking about?

"We know there are lean times, Mother, but if a man enjoys his work, money isn't all that important."

"And does my daughter-in-law agree with you that money isn't important?" Gram said testily.

"Well, of course it's important," Sara's mother put in placatingly. "But a happy man is a good husband. It's better to have a happy husband than a rich one."

"How would you know about that?" Gram snapped.

"Mother!"

"I'm sorry, but you two ought to remember that when you started out, times weren't as difficult as they are now. You had bills to pay, but they didn't amount to as much as they do now. Don't tell me we aren't all tightening our belts a lot these days."

"Yes, but—" Sara's father tried to cut her off.

"Those children today have an even bleaker future to face with the economy as it is. Maybe Jeff's smart to be looking for a better way." Gram was definitely upholding Jeff's side, Sara realized. And Gram usually saw things the way they really were, not with the idealism some other people had. "He knows good and well that if the small-time fisherman doesn't catch the fish, the commercial fisheries will! So why shouldn't he look for something better?"

"Well, of course it's his decision, but I for one was glad to see that Sara wasn't swayed to want to give up the kind of life we've tried to teach her is the best way." Her father sounded downright self-righteous, Sara thought. And what did he mean? The kind of life that's the best way? The kind of life they had? She turned away, thinking that it would look bad if they all decided to come out of the parlor and discovered her eavesdropping.

Their voices faded into the background as she walked down the hall toward the kitchen, deep in thought. Gram had said they were all tightening their belts. She hadn't noticed, she realized with a pang. She'd been complaining about silly things like the pink blouse, and hadn't even noticed others in the family were going without, too. Now that she thought about it, there were a lot more meatless meals lately. She hadn't minded, because she wasn't a big meat eater, but she guessed now that that had been due to the tightened financial situation of the family. And she hadn't seen her dad drinking any beer in a while. Foolishly she'd thought it was because he'd decided to lighten up, but maybe that had been a major cutback instead.

Well, she thought dispiritedly as she looked through the refrigerator, it seemed Jeff had been right all along. Fishing didn't appear to be the way to go if you were starting out in life right now. But that still didn't give him the right to attack her dad. He couldn't just pull up stakes and move the whole family off the island and look for a job. That was stupid! He wasn't qualified for anything else. What kind of job did Jeff expect him to get? No, for her father, fishing was the only answer. And Jeff shouldn't have brought him into the picture. It seemed to Sara that Jeff owed them all an apology. But after last night she wondered if he'd ever speak to their family again!

One thing was for sure, though: He wouldn't be coming to pick her up for school today. And that meant that from now on there would be a great big hole in her life.

The sound of footsteps told her someone was coming. She busied herself starting breakfast and acted surprised when her mother came in the room.

"Oh, Sara! I didn't know you were down already." Her mom looked at her oddly, and began dragging out frying pans.

"Yeah, well, I am," Sara returned lamely. "Where's Gram and Dad?"

"They're in the parlor discussing something," her mother said vaguely. "Uh, Sara . . ." she went on, and Sara knew exactly what was coming next.

"Mom, I don't want to talk about it," she said firmly.

Her mother looked surprised, and a little annoyed. "Well, I think you should," she said with asperity. "That boy said a few things last night that he shouldn't have—"

Sara was close to tears. "Mom! I don't want to talk about it, okay?" she almost shouted.

"But—"

Sara turned and ran out of the room. "You all shouldn't have been eavesdropping. It's my business," she cried, and raced upstairs. She wouldn't have any breakfast. She'd throw it up, anyway. Hurriedly she grabbed a sweater before running back downstairs. Someone had placed her school things on the small table in the hall, and she collected them quickly.

"I'm going to Susy's," she called, and was out the door and running before anyone could answer.

By the time she got to Susy's her heart was pounding and her face was wet with tears. She stopped to dry it off hastily with a Kleenex before walking up the porch steps.

Susy was shocked to see Sara. "What are you doing here?"

"What do you mean? Can't a friend walk with you to the bus stop?" Sara answered shortly.

"Well, I mean, uh . . . Jeff . . . Didn't you . . . ? What happened?" Susy was dumbfounded and still stood in front of Sara without inviting her in.

Sara pushed past her and snapped, "I don't want to talk about it. Just consider that chapter in my life closed." Her expression told volumes.

Susy looked at her and nodded. "Okay," she said uncertainly. She hesitated a moment and then started toward her kitchen. "Come on. There's extra hot cocoa and oatmeal if you want."

"Thanks." Sara followed her back but declined to eat anything.

When they got to the bus stop, Jeff was already there. Sara faced in the exact opposite direction from him. She wouldn't let him have the satisfaction of seeing how miserable she was. She halted several feet from the actual bus stop and made Susy wait with her until it came down the road. They got on last and sat in total silence all the way to school. Sara could hear talk from the back, low confidential talk, as if the speakers didn't want anyone else in the bus to hear them. She identified the voices as belonging to Jackie and Stan. Occasionally Jeff muttered something, but Sara had no idea what the conversation was about.

All during school Sara felt everyone's eyes were on her. Surely by now it was news that they weren't a twosome anymore. Whether anyone actually noticed or not, she didn't know, but when it came time to ride the bus home again, she found out what Stan Love thought of the breakup. As he boarded the bus she heard him yell to some of his buddies who rode other buses, "Hey! It's party time tonight. Jeff's a bachelor again and the guys are gonna howl!"

Sara sank down in her seat and tried to pretend she didn't hear that horrible announcement. There was a buzz from the back of the bus as several people, all males, made remarks to Jeff.

She heard Jeff say something that sounded like a swear word followed by "Shut up!" That confused her. Did it mean he didn't like being "free" again? Well, if he didn't, she decided he could make the first move. After all, he'd been the first one to start the argument with his insults.

Jackie got on the bus right after Stan, and as she passed Sara's seat she paused. "Sara, Jeff has organized a car wash to help raise money to buy sports equipment next year. It's next Saturday. Are you going to come?" She sounded like she actually cared whether Sara was going to show up or not.

Sara tried to cover up her surprise at hearing about this for the first time. She'd known that Jeff was really concerned about the sports-equipment cutback, had written that editorial about it, but it was news to her that he'd actually decided to do something constructive about it.

"Uh, no, I don't think so," she said lamely, and shrank back more in her seat as Jackie gave her a strange look.

After she'd passed on by and was somewhere in the back of the bus, Susy snorted, "Boy, she's sure making sure the coast is clear fast, isn't she?"

"What do you mean?" Sara asked listlessly.

"I mean she's checking to see if you and Jeff are really on the outs or not, and since you won't be at the car wash, she's taking that as an all-clear sign." Susy talked in the tone of voice she used when she baby-sat incredibly dull kids.

It annoyed Sara. "Well, it is!" she snapped, and stuck her nose in a book to keep from having to talk any more on the way home.

When she walked in the house there was more discussion going on in the parlor, but this time the subject didn't seem to be Jeff.

"I think it would work. We'd rearrange some of the furniture in the living room and bring all your things down here," Sara's mother was saying.

"Well," Gram said slowly, "I don't want to put you to all that trouble, but if it wasn't for her—"

Sara pushed the half-open door wider and walked in, halting the conversation.

"Oh, Sara!" her mother exclaimed. She waved a hand at the parlor and asked, "What do you think of moving Gram down here and separating you girls?"

"You mean I'd get a room of my own?"

"Yes. And it's about time, too," Gram said firmly. "You girls need space of your own."

"Yes," Sara agreed. A place to cry in peace! She looked around the parlor. "Can I help get it ready?"

Gram laughed and looked at Sara's mother. "There, does that answer your questions?"

Mrs. Wilson smiled. "I think you're right. I'll go get Tom and we'll all get started."

"Dad's home?" Sara asked. Her dad was always fishing until dark these days. "Why isn't he out on the boat?"

Her mother sent a warning look at Gram, who'd opened her mouth. Sara caught it and felt pricklings of anxiety.

"He's home today," her mom said matter-of-factly. "Didn't think there was any reason to go out. Word's out the fish aren't running, so why waste the gas?" She moved briskly toward the door, tapping Sara's shoulder. "Why don't you run and change and we'll get to work."

"Okay," Sara said, and went upstairs. But as she changed into an old pair of jeans, she thought about her dad's not going out fishing today. As far as she knew, he never failed to at least make a try of it. But the more she thought about it, the more she realized that even though he had been going out recently, she didn't think he'd brought a catch home for quite a while. She'd been so wrapped up in her big romance with Jeff that she'd been practically oblivious of everything around her. Well, she thought, smiling sadly, now that the big romance was over, she'd have all the time in the world to get back in touch with her family and what was happening to it.

They moved Gram that very night, and the next weekend Sara was in her own room, with Joy down the hall in Gram's old one. Joy was thrilled because now she could leave her toys all over without fearing that Sara would crush one. But she was unhappy, too, because in the past she could count on Sara to pick up at least half of them. Now it was all her responsibility to keep the room neat, a point her mother made to her strongly. "You're a big girl now, young lady, and you won't be able to sucker your sister into doing your work for you."

Sara, hearing the conversation in the other room, looked at her own room, which now seemed so empty. She'd have to do something to make it seem less abandoned, she supposed, but she really didn't care at the moment. It could stay that way. It would match her life. Empty. Abandoned.

Even worse was the knowledge that while she sat in her half-empty room there were probably all kinds of kids in town at the car wash helping out for their school. And no doubt Jeff was in charge of it all, overseeing the work, making sure the customers were happy. He was probably recording everything that happened so he could write another article for the paper, Sara thought a little sourly. Well, he could have his paper. And he could go to college and turn into the most famous reporter the world ever saw, for all she cared! And then she broke down and cried. Her first good cry in her very own room. Somehow it didn't give her as much satisfaction as she'd always expected it would.

During the next two weeks she did more crying than she thought a person was entitled to during one lifetime. It seemed that Jeff didn't spend his time pining away for her lost company. He sat with Jackie on the bus from then on. To Sara, that was the final insult. If he'd sat with the guys, at least she'd have felt he was as miserable as she was. Not only did he sit with another girl, he seemed to be really enjoying it. They had an endless string of things to talk about, in low voices that no one could hear. And they found an awful lot of things to laugh over. Every time Sara saw them, she felt a stabbing pain in her heart.

Susy noticed, too. And being Susy, of course she couldn't keep quiet about it.

On the way home from the bus stop one afternoon, as Sara noticed Jeff walking Jackie home, Susy started in on him.

"Well, he sure didn't leave your spot empty long enough to get cold. Look at the two of them. Have you noticed they seem to be together all the time lately? I mean, during class, after class, on the bus, at lunch. Everywhere!"

Sara didn't want to hear about it. She cut Susy off with what she hoped would be a conversation ender. "And do you blame him? What guy could resist her? She's pretty. She's in most of his classes, so they have more in common—"

"How can you talk about her like that?" Susy flared. "Sometimes I don't understand you, Sara. You should be mad at her for stealing him. You know, I always thought your father was being silly when he said you didn't have a jealous bone in your body. But he's right. You should be jealous now! Get mad! It's not normal to act like you do."

"Well, who says a person has to be normal anyway?" Sara muttered, and stalked away from Susy toward her house.

Honestly! she thought. Sometimes Susy was downright unbearable. Why was she so vindictive? You'd think Jeff had dumped her, not Sara. And she shouldn't blame Jackie. If Jeff had a decent bone in his body, he could have resisted Jackie's attraction. He could have come to Sara anytime during the last two weeks and made up with her if he wanted to. It was obvious he didn't want to.

And Susy was wrong about Jackie setting out to steal Jeff. Wasn't she?

The next few days at school Sara found herself watching Jackie and Jeff with the avid interest of a Peeping Tom. She couldn't prevent herself from doing it. She was disgusted with herself for wanting to see how they got along, but it was as if they were magnets that just naturally drew her gaze. It seemed to Sara that Jackie was a downright flirt. When she laughed up into Jeff's eyes, she seemed so obvious about it, Sara couldn't understand why Jeff didn't see through her. She laughed too loud, and Sara didn't like the way she flipped her hair back from her eyes. Why didn't she just get it cut so she could see without having to go through all that trouble? And she had curves, all right. Because she was probably overweight by at least five pounds. And besides that . . .

Sara stopped dead in her tracks in the middle of the hallway as she was changing classes and realized just how she'd been thinking. She was no better than Susy! And that wasn't the way she'd been brought up. She was being totally unfair to Jackie, and she knew it. And all because Susy kept making her snide little remarks. Maybe Susy was a bad influence. Maybe Susy wasn't even a good friend. Sara considered trying to change Susy, but the mere thought of taking on that project exhausted her. Lately all she wanted to do was lie around her room staring at nothing. It took less energy, and no one seemed to mind. Now that Joy was out of her room, she had all the peace she wanted in the world. And nothing to do with it.

# 11

May ended and June came. Though it had been only a few weeks since their argument, Sara felt like it was a lifetime. Looking in the mirror one morning, she was almost sure she saw age lines. I've grown old before my time, she thought. But those little creases under her eyes were really from not sleeping too well anymore. Tension had grown in the house that colored everything anyone did. Her parents snapped at the children and each other, Joy didn't laugh as much, and Gram seemed to be spending more and more time in her room downstairs—more than she'd ever spent upstairs. When Ruth commented on it, Gram tried to convince her it was because her arthritis had made it difficult for her to mount the stairs, so she'd not gone up to her room a lot of times when she would have liked to.

"Now that it's so handy, I go in there to get away from it all," Gram maintained.

She hadn't bothered to explain what "it all" was, but Sara knew. It was this feeling of gloom that seemed to saturate the very air. Sara had tried to figure out just exactly what was causing the problem, but had failed until she overheard her parents talking one night in their room. It was late, and Sara had walked barefoot to the bathroom, but halted before going in. The door to her parents' room across the hall had stood slightly ajar, enough for the sound of low conversation to escape.

"Ruth, what can I say? We'll just have to tighten our belts a little more and look for more ways to economize." Sara thought her father sounded so tired. The kind of tiredness that came when you strove to do something and were continually defeated.

"But we've tightened our belts and economized to the point where we're down to bare bones!" Ruth sounded angry, but whether she was angry at her husband or life, Sara didn't know.

"We've seen this happen before and we've gotten through it. Fishermen's lives are filled with lean and fat times, you know that," Tom said with exaggerated patience.

"But have the lean times been this long? Almost a full year since anyone's had a really big catch?" Now Ruth sounded on the verge of tears, and Sara hurt for her mother.

"What am I supposed to do about it?" Sara's father asked, his voice rising with exasperation. She flinched as if he'd spoken to her in that tone instead of to her mother.

"I'm not asking you to do anything more than what you are doing now—trying to catch fish. But at least let me try to find a part-time job. I may not have any skills, but I could punch keys at the market. They've advertised for a—"

"Now, don't start that again," Sara's father said tiredly.

"But—"

No! No wife of mine is ever going to work." Her
ther's voice had a steely inflexibility.

"Then why have you let me go clamming from time
to time?"

"Oh, Ruth, you know that's not the same thing. Just
turn out the light," he said in a tone of voice that
sounded almost threatening. "Go to sleep."

As silently as possible, Sara entered the bathroom,
not letting the door click. It seemed Jeff had really called
this one, she thought with remorse. It looked like her
parents had been conspiring to hide the real state of
things from their children. Maybe they'd been afraid
to worry them. Their silence had worked. Now Sara was
almost sorry she'd heard them talking.

Another thing that happened in June that bothered
Sara had to do with Susy. She and Susy had still been
walking to the bus stop every schoolday and riding together. They'd shared some classes together and eaten
lunch together, but they were joined now by the friends
Susy had made when she'd been forced to sit elsewhere
while Sara had Jeff. Now there were five of them and
Sara felt left out. At first she didn't mind. She was so
sunk in a world of her own misery that she hadn't minded
that the other four always had something to talk and
laugh about. She just sat there at the table and quietly
and unenthusiastically ate whatever the school cooks
dished out. On weekends, too, she and Susy hadn't done
much. It seemed Susy never asked her to go anywhere,
and Sara hadn't asked Susy to do anything with her.
She'd rather sit in her lonely room with her lonely
thoughts.

Sara's mother announced one morning, "The family
needs an outing. I propose we pack a lunch and make
a day of the celebration in Beaufort." Every June, the
nearby town of Beaufort celebrated the reenactment of
a pirate invasion.

That made Sara remember all the times in the past when she and Susy had attended the reenactment together, either with one of their parents or with other kids. Here it was mid-June and neither of them had said a thing about it. Probably Susy thought Sara wasn't interested, Sara thought. I've been a regular hermit! And that wasn't good. It had to stop. It was time for her to get up off her rear and get back to living. It was obvious that living had to be without Jeff in the picture, but if she didn't watch it, it would be without *anyone* in the picture. With this revelation, Sara went to the phone. She'd call Susy right away and invite her to come with the family. Seeing Susy would help take her mind off things, just like old times.

The first thing Susy said was, "I can't." She sounded downright happy about it.

"Why not?"

They were talking on the phone, but Sara didn't need to see Susy's face as she made her next announcement to know her friend was really pleased with herself.

" 'Cause I'm going with Don."

"Don who?"

"Don Scott," Susy said with impatience. "He's asked me to go with him this year. We're joining some of his friends on a float. I think he likes me. Honestly, Sara, don't you remember he asked me to go out with him a couple of weeks ago?"

He had? And Susy had told Sara all about it? Sara felt terrible. She didn't remember any such thing. Where had her head been? "Oh, well, uh, that's great." She mustered as much enthusiasm as she could, despite her stupefaction.

"Yeah, if it hadn't been for Marsha and Trish, I wouldn't have gotten the first date."

"How's that?" Sara asked before she realized what a mistake that was.

"Huh?" Then Susy exploded. "Sara Wilson! Don't

you remember me telling you they gave me some hints on how to act around boys? How I should be more cheerful and all? If you weren't so wrapped up in your own problems, you would have listened to me," she almost shrieked. "But all you've been thinking about is yourself. It's time for you to face the fact that you've lost Jeff and get back to the living. Find another boy!"

Susy hung up and Sara recoiled from the sound of the receiver slamming down on the other end.

She stared at it for what seemed like an eternity. Susy was right, she thought with a deep pain inside. She'd been so upset by the big "dump-Sara" scene, she'd lost touch with her friend. And now it looked like she didn't have that friend anymore.

She had to fix things fast. Quickly she dialed Susy's number. Susy got it on the seventh ring; it was as if she knew who it would be and had almost not answered it at all.

"Susy! I'm so sorry!" Sara apologized before Susy could hang up again. "Really, I am. You're absolutely right. I have been thinking about only myself. But, uh, that's going to stop now." She hoped! "I . . . uh . . . was wondering if maybe I could go with you guys to the reenactment?" Her voice was all quivery. Susy hadn't said anything and Sara was afraid she'd really done it with her dumb act before.

There was a long sniff from the other end. "That's okay. I . . . I really felt bad about what I said to you a while ago, Sara." Sara realized Susy had been crying. She was as sorry about the argument as Sara was. "But, uh, I . . . Well, you won't exactly fit in. I mean, the kids are kind of like on Noah's ark—you know, two by two? And, uh . . ."

"Oh." Sara saw it clearly. She would be an odd number.

"But you could come anyway. Don and I will just include you—"

"No, that's okay. I would feel out of place, but, uh, thanks anyway. For caring." Her voice dropped off, as suddenly she realized just what a loner she was turning into.

After some more small talk, during which it was obvious both girls were a little embarrassed, Sara hung up and walked upstairs to her room, reflecting on the mess she'd managed to get herself into. Now she really didn't feel much like attending the reenactment.

The town of Beaufort would be staging a pirate invasion like one that had happened back in 1747. Men dressed up in pirate outfits—or as close as they could come—and there was a fight at sea between two pretend pirate ships. There would be a cannon blast and the men would wade ashore and chase after women from the town, who were dressed up in old-fashioned clothes too. It was usually a lot of fun and everyone had a great time. But this year it was going to be the pits, Sara thought. She wondered if Jeff's family would go. They always did. Practically everyone did.

Her mother seemed bent on trying to infuse the day with gaiety. She packed a huge lunch that Sara was sure used up the grocery money for the month. The five of them piled into the battered old Ford and headed for town.

Sara sat next to the window in back with Joy and Gram. She really wished she could find some other kids to hang out with today, but she was afraid Susy was right: all the kids seemed to come in pairs lately. One thing she was going to have to work on was finding some new friends or cultivating some old ones. There were a couple of girls she'd been fairly close to in grade school and she knew they still liked her. Starting with school in the fall, Sara resolved, she was going to widen her circle of friends. No matter what happened with a boy in the future, she needed friends to fall back on and talk to when times got rough. Making this decision helped a little, but there was still a funny little ache in her heart.

She looked out at the day. It had to be wonderful weather, she thought dejectedly. The sky was blue and clear. Sara's favorite wildflowers beside the road waved their heads in the breeze as the car rolled past dandelions, Queen Anne's lace, and blue cornflowers. But seeing them failed to lift her mood. All the way across the inlet, Sara stared into space, seeing Jeff instead of the beautiful coastal area she lived in.

Then something her father said to her mother grabbed her attention.

"Jim says he heard a report yesterday about someone catching speckled trout at the Cape. And he's heard bluefish are running." There was a touch of jubilation in his voice that made Ruth respond in kind.

She touched his arm and almost whispered, "Is it true?"

"Hope so. Can't imagine anyone lying. Guess I'll take a run out there early tomorrow."

He sounded carefree, and Sara knew the news about fish running had lightened the mood in the family. She was glad for the others, but for herself she didn't care. I need more than a few fish to make me happy, she thought.

When they reached Beaufort and parked, Sara found out to her horror that her parents had made plans to join up with the Moores. Sara had expected Jeff to be with his friends, so when she saw him with his family waiting for hers, she began to get uptight.

"Hi," he greeted her, and she realized it was the first time they'd spoken since their big fight.

She was torn between wanting to throw herself into his arms and wanting to keep back and force him to apologize. "Hi," she managed to say without revealing anything of what she was feeling.

They began walking with the others, not talking as they made their way to Front Street, where the old-homes tour that went along with the reenactment was scheduled to begin. During the day everyone toured the fine old historical houses in Beaufort, along with the maritime museum. The locals knew the tour by heart, but it was traditional. Then, about six-thirty in the afternoon, the pirates would invade. Everyone wanted a good vantage point from which to view that, and it wasn't easy to get. The reenactment was a tourist-drawing event that filled the town with hordes of visitors. The merchants enjoyed the added business.

They were a block away from Front Street when Gram suddenly stopped and began going through her purse. "Well," she said in agitation, "I can't find my aspirin."

"What's that?" Ruth stopped and looked at her.

"My aspirin. You know, for my arthritis," Gram explained.

"Is it flaring up?"

"No, but if it does, I want to be prepared." Gram's eyes focused on Sara. "Would you and Jeff go to the drugstore and get me some?"

"Oh, I have some in my purse," Doris Moore said, but Gram shushed her.

"I have to have a special brand. The kind with the coating on it so it won't irritate my stomach."

"Oh," Doris said, enlightenment coloring her voice.

Sara wanted to sink through the concrete walk. Gram was scheming! And right in front of Jeff! What did he think? She was afraid to look.

But surprisingly he took her arm and said, "Sure, Gram, we'd be glad to go. What brand is it?"

"Oh, Sara knows."

"Okay." Jeff pulled on Sara, making her follow him as he headed off to town. But as soon as she turned to walk with him, he dropped her arm.

She felt even worse then. It was bad enough Gram had to throw them together, but now it seemed obvious he'd gone along with it just to be nice to Gram. The idea of being with Sara was as appealing to him as getting second-degree sunburn.

They walked in silence for a while. Both of us know darn well that it doesn't take two to buy a bottle of aspirin, Sara thought resentfully. Why did Gram have to do that! She'd thought her grandmother was smarter than that, and more considerate.

Well, it was a sure thing that they couldn't keep up this silence. One of them was going to have to break it.

"I overheard Dad tell Mom that your father said someone caught some trout," she commented.

"Yeah, so he tells me," Jeff returned, and Sara noted that he didn't sound as annoyed about that topic as he used to.

They walked a few more steps, and neither spoke again. As they rounded a corner, Sara almost tripped over her own feet. Jackie was on the opposite side of the street, but the thing that really shocked Sara was that a guy from the senior class was walking with her and they had their arms around each other.

Oh, no, she thought. Had Jackie dumped Jeff? If he saw her, he'd feel so hurt! Sara had to do something to keep him from seeing them.

But it was too late.

"Hi, guys," Jackie called cheerfully and distinctly across the street. No avoiding that, or her big wave.

Sara waved back weakly, feeling Jeff's pain. But when she glanced at him, he was smiling at Jackie and waving too. The guy with Jackie nodded and smiled; then the two of them moved on. Jeff kept on walking, his expression totally blank. Either he was a good actor and could hide his emotions, or he didn't care about Jackie. Sara was totally confused. Wasn't he upset about some other guy moving in on his territory? Or hadn't they been dating all that time since she and Jeff broke up? Wasn't that the reason she'd seen them together, so cozy in the library at school and on the bus? Sara puzzled over that for about sixty seconds more and then couldn't keep quiet about it.

"Uh, Jeff?"

"Yeah?"

"Is Jackie dating that guy?"

"Yeah, why?" He didn't sound in the least concerned. Like she'd asked him about the weather.

"Oh," she said in a small voice. "How long has that been going on?"

"A couple of months, I guess."

Now Sara was really confused. She just had to ask, "So why did you two seem to be together so much? I mean, I saw you a couple of times in the library, and every time you were on the bus, you really had your heads together." Sara tried to sound nonchalant. She'd die if Jeff knew how she really felt.

"Oh, that. We got assigned to be partners on an English project. We had to research religion's part in the historic development of government in Europe," he explained in the dry, crackly voice of a creaky old college professor. "Man, did we hate that project. But Jackie's got such a good sense of humor she made it seem funny. She wanted to rename it religion's role in the hysteric development of Europe. I don't think Mrs. Fulton saw too much humor in it, but at least we got it done. Got only a B-minus, but I don't care. It was a boring project."

He continued walking, and they turned another corner and started up the street toward the drugstore. They were like salmon trying to swim upstream. Everyone was headed toward Front Street and they were headed away from it. The later you came, the farther away you had to park, so there was a constant stream of visitors for them to wade through.

As she walked, Sara thought about what Jeff had said. It seemed that even during the time Jackie and Jeff were working on the English project, she'd really been dating that senior. So it looked like Jeff hadn't filled Sara's empty spot with anyone. She took a deep breath. Here goes, she thought.

"Jeff, there's something I'd like to say."

Her serious tone made him stop walking and turn to look down at her. His expression told her nothing, which didn't make things any easier for Sara. She had to go on her own courage.

"Yeah?" he prompted.

"I apologize for blowing up at you that night," she said with a rush of air from her lungs. "I shouldn't have said all those stupid things about newspapers and you being a reporter. They weren't true. I don't know why I said them. I guess . . . I guess the way you talked about my dad made me feel hurt."

Jeff opened his mouth, but Sara hurried on; once she got going, she had to keep going or she'd lose her nerve.

"I really have been thinking about what you said. You know, about the bad times when a fisherman can't make ends meet? Well, it's been like that for us—"

"It's been like that for all the fishermen on the island," Jeff managed to put in.

"Yeah, well, I guess I wasn't aware of it because my folks tried to keep it from us." She went on to tell him about the conversation she'd overheard one night. "So you were right all along. I had my head in the sand and I liked it that way. I guess I had these rosy little visions of what my life was going to be like in the future, and I didn't like it when you said things that would force me to come out of my dream world. I was afraid to do that. The night of the argument you forced me to really look at some things and I was so scared I guess I struck out at you. Jeff . . ." Her breath came almost like a sob. "I'm so sorry. That's all I can say." She ended with a shrug.

Jeff's face broke into a big smile. "Thanks, Sara. It means a lot to me that you can apologize for your part in that dumb argument. I have to apologize for my part, too. I don't know what happened. It was like the arms race. Once we got started, things kept getting worse. Afterward, I really felt bad about what I'd said to you. All the way home I kept telling myself I was a creep and I ought to walk right back and apologize. But I guess some of the things you said made me so mad I couldn't do it right away. Then the next day you wouldn't even look at me. You seemed so . . . I don't know. So far away after that. Like if you never had anything to do with me again, it would be too soon." He looked down at his sneakers. "And you're not selfish. I'm especially sorry about that." He looked earnestly into her eyes.

"That's okay," Sara replied huskily. "I said a few rotten things too."

"But you said some true things, too. Like, if I want college I should be willing to work a little harder for it. When I came to your place, I was just angry at life and at my dad for making it so tough for me to get what I wanted." He took Sara's arm and began walking slowly down the street again. They crossed the street and then Jeff continued. "You know, I felt a little disloyal for not wanting to do what Dad expected of me, and even worse for not telling him. I guess knowing what his reaction was going to be when I finally did tell him made me a little slow about approaching him. So I kept the whole thing to myself until that day we argued. His reaction was just as bad as I expected, and it put me in such a lousy mood that when I got to your place I blew up at you." He stopped and took Sara's shoulders in his hands. "After that fight, I figured my bad mood had ruined it for us forever." He looked at her in a way that made her knees weak. Maybe there was a chance for them after all.

"Well, I understand it all now. And you said some things that were true about me, too." She gave a short laugh. "I've had plenty of time to think lately, and I realized what you said about me not liking change was probably because of the way my parents brought me up. You know, Dad's so old-fashioned. I think it's been drilled into my head that a woman's place is in the home. But it's a big modern world out there, isn't it? Time to give up all those old-fashioned values. Time for me to learn new ways of thinking. And accept them. Like college for you. It's right for you and you should have it." She looked at him shyly. "Could you tell me again about your plans, like what you'd take?"

"I'd major in journalism, which would mean I'd have to take a lot of English and communications courses. Computers, media, things like that. I'm really looking forward to it." His whole face shone with anticipation.

"What about a scholarship?"

"Well, you remember I said there might be a couple I could get? I still had a problem with extra costs, like transportation and all. But Mr. Thomas told me about this loan I could get for my education that I'd have to repay once I graduated. I didn't like that idea, because Dad's always had this thing about not getting anything on credit. He's always saying, 'If we can't afford to pay for it with cash, then we can do without it.' " Jeff grimaced. "I guess I had the same kind of thinking. But Mr. Thomas told me if I want college I have to change my thinking, so I talked it out with Dad. Showed him all the facts on paper that Mr. Thomas wrote up for me. We had some session!" He smiled and shrugged.

"But in the end, Dad and I agreed we'd go for it. I'll have to shoulder the responsibility of repaying the loan, Dad said. So I will!" He looked so confident and happy, as if he could see his future clearly and wasn't afraid of it.

Sara's old fear resurfaced and she decided now was the time to voice it.

Her cheeks turned red as she made the next admission. "I was against the idea of you going to college because I was afraid of losing you. I saw college as something that would take you away from here. From me." She tried to make it a joke. "I guess I've gotten used to your face. Would you move off the island and leave . . . everyone when you became a reporter?" No matter how she tried, all her anxiety came out in her voice, and her words were shaky.

Pedestrians were milling past them, making it difficult to keep the conversation going without constant interruptions, so Jeff took her hand and pulled her forward. They walked along the curb, with him talking over his shoulder at her as she followed.

"Sara, I really do love this place. I wouldn't want to forget it. I did grow up here. I'm going to the nearest extension of the university so I can come home a lot. And after college . . . well, I'd have to move wherever there was a job opportunity." He turned to face her, and she almost walked right into his arms. "But you wouldn't lose me. If you didn't want to, that is . . . if you still want me." His expression told her he hoped that was the answer she wanted.

It was.

She smiled shyly. "I still want you, Jeff." If she'd wanted to say much more, she couldn't have, because it's impossible to talk when someone's kissing you. When they stopped it was to find all the people around them observing them with various reactions—smiles, frowns,

and shaking of heads. Sara giggled in spite of her embarrassment.

"I won't think of your going off to college as a threat
now," she said happily. "Instead I'll think of how much
college will improve your mind. And you can teach me
all the things you learn." She smiled at a couple that
passed close by. They were dressed in the period cos-
tumes they'd wear later. The man would play a pirate
who would kidnap the woman. Sara pointed after the
couple. "I've already learned something. See them?
Well, the clothes they're wearing and the pirate ships
and the life-style from back in the 1700's are long gone,
because things have to change. And the way my dad
thinks has to change too. But even if he doesn't grow
and change, I'm going to." She gazed up into Jeff's face,
and then shrieked as he swooped her up into his arms.
He looked around them.

"There are too many people around here," he muttered.

He walked over to a doorway that was recessed from
the sidewalk and put his arms tightly around Sara. Gazing
down into her eyes, he went on in a teasing voice, "I'm
sure glad to hear about the *new* Sara. Will she be my
*new* girl so we can have a *new* start?"

Sara stood on tiptoes. "I'd love to be your new girl,
Jeff," she whispered, right before they kissed.

Gram had to wait an awfully long time for her aspirin.

Look out for some more MAGIC MOMENTS in your life:

**LIGHTNING BOOKS**